Be My Angel

Merideth was searching for answers,
but would she like what she found?

Harriet Canne

a sycamore tree book

from

Pacific Press® Publishing Association
Nampa, Idaho
Oshawa, Ontario, Canada

Edited By Jerry D. Thomas
Designed by Dennis Ferree
Cover art by Katie Atkinson

Copyright © 1999 by
Pacific Press® Publishing Association
Printed in the United States of America
All Rights Reserved

Library of Congress Cataloging-in Publication Data

Canne, Harriet, 1965-
    Be my angel / Harriet Canne.
        p.   cm.
    ISBN 0-8163-1708-9 (paper)
    I. Title.
PS3554.E4953B4 1999
813'.54—dc21   98-52825
                                                            CIP

99 00 01 02 03 • 5 4 3 2 1

Harriet Canne is a psuedonym.
The author lives in northern California
and works for a newspaper.

The right way to wholeness is made up,
unfortunately, of fateful detours and wrong
turnings . . . a path whose
labyrinthine twists and turns are not
lacking in terrors.

—Carl Jung

CHAPTER
1

Monday was always a busy one at my real estate office. Back before everything came crashing, smashing, cascading down.

See, all week long people want their real estate agent to take them around to tour this house and that house—oh yes, and the darling, little poopsy house over there, the one with the cute, cute, cute Victorian porch.

They want to snoop around and point at shadows in the corners of the ceiling and pop off remarks like, "Say, look at those water spots," and they'll make faces and then, of course, they want to bargain for a lower selling price.

They want to poke around in the closets and complain that they're much too teeny-tiny small and try to convince themselves that there's a funny odor, "Does carbon monoxide have a smell?" and then haggle, haggle, haggle.

They want to count the electrical outlets in the downstairs bathroom and come up short by about two dozen—and tell you what a trashy place it is, but they want it anyway, if there's a price adjustment. You know, wiggle room. Everybody's looking for wiggle room.

Then they want to sit around in the office and make small talk and speculate and prognosticate about the future of mortgage rates and burn up time until you've only got five minutes until your next appointment for your next set of clients who are going to do the same thing all over again.

So Monday was always catch-up day. Putting-out-fires day. Taking-care-of-business day. Real estate is a cutthroat business. Gotta stay on your toes.

On that Monday in March, there I was plopped behind my desk, the phone ringing, my reading glasses on, my pulse rate up. When I finally picked up the phone, it was the same hotshot lawyer out of San Francisco squawking at me, wanting to close up on the same deal for the same parcel of land just outside of town:

Home builder's dream
Just off Hwy. 1, private drive, beautiful 5.5 acre piece of heaven, ocean view. Historic one-room schoolhouse on site, water not a problem. Zoned residential. Must see to believe.
Call Merideth Dill Real Estate.

Ownership on this land was held in a family trust, and the trustee, an elderly woman out on the East Coast, was looking to sell.

On this nice five-and-a-half-acre plot, Mr. Bernard Hunt was probably looking to erect a gigantic, tacky weekend getaway. Probably wanted pink stucco with hints of Spain and the Mediterranean. He might even begin construction and the bulldozers would roar and the cement trucks would rumble . . . until he would hit up against the Green Ash Planning Commission, who would tell him exactly the style he could—and could not—build. Community standards and all that.

Mediterranean was out.

Spain? No way. Forget about it.

The only style that worked here was a sort of austere Victorian throwback. East Coast salt blocks or eco-style, severely weathered sea ranch structures.

This fella, though, he had no time for instruction from me. And on he went, his voice growing higher and tighter. His blood pressure was restricting the flow of oxygen to his brain.

I had told him, I told this Mr. Bernard Hunt, Esq., of San Francisco, more times than I could count that escrow takes time. Thirty to forty days in some cases. I've seen escrow take three months—and then fall through. There are steps, there are reports, that must be completed. Even so, he kept phoning from his yacht in Half Moon Bay. Day after day. Showing off to his twenty-eight-year-old girl-

Chapter 1

friend the whole time. Some folks think that pushing your real estate agent around is some kind of show of force. Muscle flexing. Whatever.

I told Mr. Bernard Hunt, E-S-Q, or E-S-P or whatever he was, that I was even at that moment reading through a report on water quality with my supermagnification bifocals on.

"Water what?" he shrieked over the static on his garbagey little cellular phone.

"Water quality," I said. "I want to make sure the water is suitable for human consumption."

There was a building, an old stone schoolhouse, on the property—it was called the Pompidou property—that had been condemned from way back.

Since the building was condemned, no one could live in it.

Still, I wanted a report on its roof, its foundation, its floors, its pretty white-washed walls and what little plumbing and electricity the structure had. I needed to know if it was under siege from termites and other creeping things. I wanted the local historical society to eyeball it to see if they'd take an owner to court who was inclined to pull the building down. You can't believe—an agent has to have a report on everything to cover her flanks. Especially when a lot of money is on the line.

I tried to tell Bernard Hunt all of that, still he muttered curses and ranted and went apoplectic and cut me off unsatisfied. As though I'd done him wrong.

The front door to the office opened. Clang, clang went the copper cowbell over the door, and I looked up, and there was my niece, Brenda Ann, standing there with her mustache and her nose ring. Brenda Ann, was my sister Peggy's girl. A middle child if there ever was one.

Of course, Brenda Ann didn't go by Brenda Ann. Big sigh. She'd come up with some other name for herself like Star Tree or Treeroot or Star Root or Rootie Toot Toot or some such.

I knew she cared about trees, as well as the coastline and the preservation of disappearing species, shrinking wetlands, and what not. She protested a fair amount and just the summer before had strapped herself to a bulldozer with bungie cords. Her picture had been in the paper.

The point is, here is a girl who could be very pretty with a little bleach on that upper lip and a quality salon perm (not for curl, just for body) and more selectivity in the clothing department. She clodded around a lot in scary black Nazi-type boots and torn Levi's and Salvation Army type tops. I don't know, is that asking too much to care about looking your best?

You want the forests to be beautiful, I had told her, but you can't spend ten minutes with a bar of lotion-based facial cleanser?

Brenda Ann needed the prayers of the community, and she needed my help.

I said How you doing? to her, and she said How you doing? to me. And she looked sort of bewitched and lost and forlorn. Not a normal Brenda Ann look. Like she had the role of a little lost orphan in a school play.

"Aunt Merideth," she said, and slugged herself onto the sofa across from my desk. "I have this assignment that's just crazy. Just totally, totally exponentially unfair."

"What class is it in?"

She made a terrible face. "Astronomy." Her tone of voice meant something more like, asphyxiation.

Astronomy questions. Well. When you're a real estate agent—I don't know what it is—people do seek you out. Who could blame little lost lambs like Brenda Ann from dropping by my sales office like that? There I was, a single gal with my own office on the better end of Main in downtown Green Ash. Green Ash being one of the more developing areas of Mendocino County in Northern California. Everybody knows that's where it's at. One time I went to London, England, for a week with my friend Shirley. And there we were on this old subway they have there when these two nice, appley-faced English businessmen were so excited to meet us when they found out we were from California. We got to talking. They told Shirley and me that they were in the business of selling automatically-opening doors, like the ones at Safeway and Target, stores like that. Apparently these two lads had come under the spell of a Rotarian from Fresno who had them convinced that Fresno—NOT Los Angeles and NOT San Francisco—was the next hot, hot, hotbed of automatic-opening door sales. And these two, nice, gullible old loons were simply wide-eyed and open-mouthed with excitement about California.

And it really struck me that even in other parts of the world, they know about California. And not only do they know about it, but they dream of it, they come from all over the world to start up businesses with dollar signs in their eyes, like the name California might as well be Oz.

Just take a left turn on the Yellow Brick Road. Here's where you'll wind up.

So I lived in the snappiest place in the world, and my office sat right there in the middle of it all. Right on Main Street next to the new 24-Hour Nautilus, where I had a membership and the newly remodeled Green Ash Gift Emporium, where they do a whopping tourist trade. And on top of that, I was a real estate agent in a town where that counted for something.

Astronomy. The stars in the sky—why not? I felt up to the task.

"What's the problem, hon?" I asked her.

"It's my teacher," she said. Actually, Brenda Ann managed to work in an expletive that I have chosen not to reproduce here. "He's such a dork." Again, I am editing.

"What's crawled up your tree?" I asked her.

"Oh—I could just punch that guy's lights out. You know? This teacher, this Mr. Hanson guy, picks me out of the whole class. There's like forty people in this class. And he picks me out of the whole class to write a five-page report."

"Just you?"

"Yeah, just me."

"Can he do that?"

Her lips bunched up, and she wiped at the bright silver ring in her nose. "I don't know. I was gonna go talk to the dean about it but—I don't know . . ." She gave a growl. "He can't do that," her hand made a quick chopping motion. "It's not fair. He can't just give me a five-page report and not give it to anyone else. He can't pick me out of the class and give me a five-page report like that"

Her eyes glared at me for a moment. "I think he's mental."

"Brenda Ann," I chided.

"What else is it? How else can you explain such behavior? He's a sociopathic . . . he's a . . . he's . . ." She ran out of words. And glanced about the office in growly anger.

"I'm sorry, sweetie. Are you sure there's not some reason?"

She shook her head, her nose slowly reddening. And when she spoke, her voice was small and broken. "No," she said, not looking at me. "And I've got four other classes and . . . I've got Brady. What . . . what am I supposed to do?"

Braden was her cute-as-a-muppet little eighteen-month-old boy. Some people, like her brother Marc, referred to little Brady as a mistake. Right to Brenda Ann's face. Like her little child was a cake that had burned in the oven. Something that didn't smell right and should be tossed out with the trash. Well, they didn't make snotty remarks like that around me. Not more than once, anyhow.

Two weeks ago, Marc was up from L.A. standing here in my office trying to win me over to his way of thinking. This is Marc, Brenda Ann's older, gifted, slick brother. Marc ran his slick hands through his slick hair—so masterfully gelled you could hear it crackle. And this young man who calls himself a born-again Christian had the nerve to suggest that Brenda Ann should give Brady to the state.

Give this child to the State of California. This was Marc's plan.

"He was conceived in sin," Marc insisted, "he's being raised by a child. Brenda Ann is nineteen. She's a child. A child raising a child. I mean, I love my sister, and I know God loves Braden, too, but really—"

I raised a hand, and my fingers grasped one side of his neck—oh, I just wanted to give that monster a good, hard squeeze!

I said to him in a calm, clenched voice, "Marc, you listen to me now. You listen. If you ever say to Brenda Ann what you just said to me . . . if you ever suggest she's unfit . . ." Right about then my teeth ground together, and I felt something like a sob in my throat. But it was anger. It was pity and sympathy for Brenda Ann, but it was also a kind of fury, because I never got the chance to be a mother myself. I had to breathe in a couple times. "So help me . . . so help me . . ." I threatened emptily.

Of course, Marc went and said his piece to Brenda Ann anyway. I wasn't there, but I heard about it.

Brenda Ann had cried when she told me about it. And I had put my arm around her skinny shoulder and said that Brady was not a mistake—the only mistake would be not to give that little rascal all the love in the world. And the second mistake would be to listen to balderdash from the likes of Marc.

"Have you talked to your teacher?" I asked her.

"You talk to him," Brenda Ann said. "I can't talk to him. I'll hit him."

"Bren—"

"I will. I swear I will. I'm so mad at him. How can I get an 'A' now? How?"

Chapter 1

"Write the paper, I guess."

"I can't write the paper. I can't!" she protested weepily. Then glared at me and finally gave in a little, "OK. I could write the paper. I could. Of course I could. But not when I'm the only one. You know? Can you imagine me sitting down and writing a paper that only I have been assigned? Me bowing down like that? Come on—this is me we're talking about." She was laughing now.

"I know, I know."

The more she talked about it, the more she got me fired up about this assignment. Brenda Ann knows how to get me going. Maybe if I were her age, maybe I'd have a nose ring and be shaking my fist at bulldozers too. Honestly. I don't know.

Her teacher was some goof named Dan Hanson. I wrote down his name and where his office was, and Brenda Ann gave me a kiss and a slap on the shoulder.

At lunchtime I was nowhere near getting caught up on all my work, but I needed a break. I turned the sign on the front door, and I hid in the back where I kept a little refrigerator. It was important to get away from the phone in the middle of the day to keep my sanity. Most times in a real estate office, what you have is a broker and then several agents and someone to answer phones. But in my place, I was broker and the agent and the receptionist and the accountant all rolled into one. Truth is, it was a lot of work.

I was proud of my work, but it took a toll. A big toll. Especially since business wasn't doing much. I was showing houses, I was placing ads in the paper, I was calling potential sellers, I was doing my research . . . and I wasn't selling a thing.

I pulled my sandwich out of the refrigerator, and I turned on the little TV to get my mind off things. On the PBS channel there was a guy who was doing one of those programs where they show you tricks on how to oil paint. And he was painting this scene: It was at night, of an old broken-down boat resting by an old broken-down pier. Its old beat-up mast leaning to one side.

I knew how that old boat felt. It looked as if it'd come in from a terrible storm. All tattered and battered.

The guy doing the show had one of those hushed voices as if he were talking about something secret and mysterious and sacred. Made me want to just doze right off.

He had a tiny brush with just a few hairs on it that he dipped into a gold paint to make individual stars in his night sky, and then he used a sponge kind of a thing where he dabbed in a Milky Way against the black of night.

Got me to thinking again about Brenda Ann and her astronomy class . . . and then my mind went way, way back.

Way back before Jesus took my Poppie . . . there was a framed religious painting that hung in one of the back rooms of our old Victorian house. (Poppie was my dad's name when I was a little girl.)

When I was little, we lived in a big old house that had four bed-rooms, we had a living room, and a dining room, and even had what they used to call a "great room." The great room had a huge fireplace and gigantic wing-back chairs. And when I was a little thing, I used to hoist myself up into one of those chairs and stare into the fire, and I'd just sit there being great. Being great in the great room.

Now this whole place is Peggy's house. Belongs to her.

There was a room toward the back of the house that I also used to like almost as much as the great room—it was my Poppie's cluttered, dimly-lighted study. It was a kind of a junk room too. Study room/junk room. It was the place we stored the old toys and the old books and newspapers and the things we'd found while wandering on the beach. Findings we could never bear to throw out, like about a hun-dred cobalt-blue bottles along the windowsill that once held elixirs for eternal youth, railroad lantern parts, a bleached-out dart board, chalky whale bones, and a whole collection of companionless boots.

There above my Poppie's huge oak desk—surrounded by all this mess—hung an age-darkened painting that my great-grandfather had used in religious tent revivals sometime after the Civil War. This was a cosmic culmination sort of scene: A family stood firmly planted on the earth—the picture was all out of proportion, because the people in this family were so big you could see the curvature of the earth at their feet. In real life, they would've been 100 miles tall.

This family—dressed in their goin'-to-church clothes—stood on the slick ball of the earth, and behind them was the blackness of space. Good old outer space just stretching backward for all time and all before-time. Somewhere out in the darkness there was the devil fly-ing around in the black part with his dinosaur-looking wings. He had a pointed nose and a scowl. Red, lizardy eyes.

In front of the family, floating at the far end of the painting, was a white-gold-brassy ball of light. And in the center of the light were little white outlined figures, who were Jesus and heavenly beings. Way out there.

This family standing on the slick ball of the earth—ma and pa and five kids—you saw them from the back, and they were all pointing up toward this glowing heavenly host.

What I always noticed, and what fascinated me about this painting, was that the family was neither in the dark of the darkness, nor were they in the light of the light. They were in an in-between place here on earth. What I also liked was how there was a golden stream of angels who were moving back and forth between the great golden place—heaven—and the family on earth.

So you have God way off in his heaven and the Devil way off in his darkness, but us humans and the angels—we're in this in-between place. Together.

"The Land of Choosing" is what my old patriarchal, old, maniacal, hugely bearded grandfather called this world. We can choose the light of heaven or the darkness of the devil. And ever since I was a little girl, I thought about those angels. Coming to us, working with us, helping us along in the Land of Choosing.

When you think about it, angels and real estate agents have a lot in common. The way I see it, we on earth are like customers who want to find a place to buy, a home to live for eternity. And you've got God way over on his patch of heaven—he's got mansions, streets of gold, and whatnot available. Then there's old Satan in his eternal darkness, and he's got a place waiting for us, too, not so nice. And the angels, they work on you. They try to sell you a property.

The Land of Choosing.

Or as my Poppie used to say, "'terror firma.'"

I guess they don't teach that kind of stuff in astronomy classes. They sure didn't teach it in real-estate school.

CHAPTER
2

It wasn't until the next day that I got around to heading out to Brenda's junior college.

Green Ash Community College, or GACC—called "Gak" by Brenda and her crew of friends—is a collection of buildings with a design that was popular in the 1970s. Low, colorless buildings with lots of raw brick. Simple. To the point. Dull as dishwater. When you're in real estate, you pay attention to these things.

Fortunately for beauty's sake, the little college was tucked away at the base of a small, sandy hill that was thick with tall, profusely needled pines.

The school is a little less than a mile from the ocean, so the air has that bracing sea-air quality. And sea gulls strutted like little naval officers at the sandy edges of the parking lot.

After consulting with a friendly young fellow who peered out at me from behind dirty blond dreadlocks and toted a skateboard covered with "Free Tibet" stickers, I found my way to the building that housed astronomy.

Dan Hanson's office was at the end of a small, dark hallway. After peering into a strip of frosted glass in his door and seeing no signs of florescent light and no movement, I almost didn't knock.

Then I heard a scuffling sound inside, and I went ahead and banged my knuckles on the door. A moment later a tall, gangly, good-looking forty-something man with a flank of disordered hair across his forehead appeared at the door. His eyes were quizzical and curious behind wire-framed glasses.

Just past him, deeper in the office, I could see a glowing computer monitor. Classical music was playing softly inside.

I introduced myself—my name meant nothing to him, and he made no effort to hide that. So I mentioned that I was Brenda Ann's aunt.

"Oh, yes," he said, and a faint look of amusement came to his face. "But she goes by ... what? Tree Star?"

"Yeah, whatever," I shook my head. "Don't get me started."

He had a fabulously boyish smile. Sparkly eyes.

I almost lost my train of thought. "Uh ... what was I saying? Oh, listen. Yes, she came by my office the other day—by the way do you have a moment?" I asked.

"Actually I'm in the middle of something."

"This won't take but a minute," I assured him.

He started to say something else, but I hushed him up. "Brenda Ann tells me she's receiving some unfair type treatment in your class, Mr. Hanson."

"I—" His eyebrows did a surprised little hop.

"She says that out of everyone in your class, she's the only one who's been assigned a five- or six-page report. Now, she is very upset—"

"Of course—"

"And as one of my nearest and dearest, I, of course, take issue with anyone who messes around with my Brenda Ann. She's my niece, and she's a single mother to boot. Did you know that?"

"Actually, yes I do ..."

"So I'm wondering what kind of agreement we—you and I—can come to on this thing. I mean, I'm not here to assign blame or to point fingers or any of that. What's the point of that? I'm a fixer-upper. You know what I mean? I mean, I just get in there and fix situations. My card," I said, tacking one last thought onto my windstorm of words. I held out the business card to him.

He nodded and squinted a bit behind his glasses and read the thing and looked up at me. "Meredith Dill Real Estate," he said. "Licensed broker."

It was the way he said it. He seemed delighted somehow. At first I couldn't tell if there was a slight hint of mockery ... but no ... he seemed genuinely pleased to be speaking with a licensed broker.

Just made me smile.

"That's right," I said. "My office is down next to the Green Ash Gift Emporium."

"Yes, yes, I see," he said. "Well, Ms. Dill, I want to be real honest with you," he said slowly.

"As opposed to lying."

"Right," he said, smiling again. Then he took a moment. He was one of these types to think before he spoke. I like that in a man. "Brenda is struggling in this class."

"You're saying she's not your star pupil," I said and laughed. "You know."

Dan Hanson's gaze was blank.

"Your star pupil," I laughed encouragingly. And maybe I laughed too loud. It was awfully quiet in that building. "Because of the astronomy thing," I said, prompting him to join in the joke.

He did smile finally, and it was very sweet, but full of embarrassment. Embarrassed for me. "Yes," he said in that slow, sleepy, kind of raspy voice of his. "She's no Galileo."

"She's no what?" I asked.

"She's no Galileo," he said, smiling.

"Is that a constellation or a . . ."

Dan Hanson's face fell a bit. And the smile pretty much went away. "No, he was an astronomer . . . in the . . . well, in the seventeenth century—doesn't matter."

"Smart fellow."

"Oh sure, yes, yes. Um, about Brenda—"

"Yeah, now what do you suppose we can do about her? 'Cause here's what I know: I know that in any situation there are fixed points and there's flexibility." I shrugged. "Fixed points are fixed points. Can't do much about them. But then again, there's sometimes flexibility. You know? Wiggle room."

"Wiggle room," he said quietly.

"Points of negotiation. Contingencies."

"I'll bet you sell a lot of houses," he said.

"I do OK."

"Well," he cleared his throat. "As I said, she's having a tough time. I think right now she's at about 43 percent."

"What's that mean?"

"That mean's she making an F."

"Youch."

"Now, I think . . . I think the point of taking a class is to actually learn the material."

"Amen!"

His neck muscles jumped. I think I startled him.

"Yes," he continued, and pulled off his glasses and rubbed the lenses on his shirt. "Uh, I don't like to just push students through and give them a passing grade and off they go. I really want them to leave with a useful knowledge of the subject. So, in Brenda's case, I gave her the option of writing a report, not only as a way of getting her—with any luck—to a D or even a C, but also so that she could grapple with astronomy at a pace that's more agreeable to her. To her schedule. This would give her the chance to read at home, to collect her thoughts a little, to . . . to take some of these things outside the classroom. I know about her little boy."

"You're giving her a second shot."

"Something like that." He put the polished glasses back on.

I was thrilled. And it was coming clear. "She's not cutting the mustard, and you're throwing out a lifeline."

"Well . . . sure. As I said—"

"No, I know what you said. I just think Brenda Ann can't get it through her noodle that someone's trying to help her out."

"That may be the situation."

"May be? May be, my foot. I know Brenda. I know her."

"I'm sure you do."

"And sometimes—she's getting better at this—but sometimes she has a real martyr complex. She's a middle child," I said, by way of explanation. "You know what I mean by that?"

"I think I do," Dan Hanson replied.

"Because, see, in her mind, she thinks she's the only one in the class who has to do this report."

"Well, no," Dan Hanson shook his head. "She's the only one I've offered this to as an option. I'm not making her do it. Writing the report is just something she can do as makeup work if she wants to bring her grade up."

"You know what, professor, this has all been a terrible, terrible misunderstanding. I am sorry to have taken up your time with all this." I was warming up to this guy. "Do you like being called professor?"

"Not really."

"Most people probably don't call you that."

"No. No one does."

"I didn't think so. You kind of twitched when I said it. You mind if I just call you Dan Hanson?"

"You could just call me Dan."

"That's seems a bit too familiar, if you don't mind," I said. "On the other hand, Mr. Hanson is a bit too formal. You know?"

"I—" he nodded a number of times. "Yes," he finished finally, laughing uncomfortably.

"OK, Dan Hanson," I stuck out my hand, grinned, and he gave it a good grip. "I am going to go have a talk with my niece, and I'll do what I can to straighten things out."

"Good."

"In the meantime you have my card, so if you need ... to ... to talk about Brenda Ann or ... you know, if you need any advice on buying a home ... you can just keep touching me."

His eyes bulged slightly. He withdrew his hand.

I laughed. "I mean you can keep in touch with—"

"Thank you."

"—with me."

"Good."

I crept out of the building. I was going to need a team of surgeons to get my foot out of my mouth. I got in the car and nearly cried I was so embarrassed.

You can keep touching me.

"Stupid, stupid," I muttered, banging my head against the steering wheel.

I don't get flustered around men like that. I don't get flustered by anyone. What in the world was that all about?

Almost ten years ago, I met and married a lovely, lonely man named Simon Ambrose Rosensinski. My secret name for him was Rose, taking it out of his middle and last names. He was my Rose. How he came into my life was so wispy and coincidental, so easy for him. So like him.

He had grown up in a little town called Hartsdale in the far western part of New York state. So far west that his sympathies lay more with Cleveland, Ohio, than with any of the large cities in New York. Eventually around the age of eighteen, he went to college in Cleveland and stayed there until he was about twenty-six.

One day—after months of feeling an itch he couldn't quite scratch—he put a bunch of belongings in his car and took a left-hand turn on the Yellow Brick Road and ended up in California. Ended up in Green Ash.

He had trained back in Cleveland as a painter, but out here he took a job on a fishing boat. Going out with the dawn, coming back to shore in the early afternoon. He told me he always said a prayer for the fish they pulled in. Just in case they hurt, in case they were afraid, in case they had souls.

My Rose is buried next to my Poppie up in the Green Ash Cemetery, which is situated on the crest of a hill near a sheep ranch that, on a clear day, gives you a view of the wide, watery pasture of the Pacific Ocean.

Someone—I think it was my sister Peggy—pointed out that the two men in my life who've meant anything to me have been named for flowers. Rose and Poppie. Is that supposed to mean something? I don't know.

Even though we married late in life—I was thirty-eight—Rose and I were going to have babies, and we were going to all go to heaven together one day. I made a number of trips to a local physician to work out all the details of late-life motherhood. Rose and I were going to be just like that family in my great-grandfather's painting. But after he was taken from me, the whole thing kind of lost its meaning.

Death was a confusing issue to me—mostly bundled up and held together with the undiluted agony of loss.

But there were the larger issues to deal with too. My Poppie didn't believe in the idea of the soul. He was firm on that one. He often quoted a passage in the Bible that said, "The dead know not anything."

But I often wondered how right he'd been. Especially after he died.

My mind always went to these thoughts when I drove on Highway 1 back into town—from the college I go right past the turnoff to the cemetery. A little dirt road.

These aren't the kind of thoughts I like to have. But I did curse God back then. I did. I lived in anger and darkness.

I was horrible and bitter when Rose died. It took a long time for him to die. And it was all so completely, completely unnecessary. There was no point to it. There was no up-side. No moral at the end of the story.

Everything I had fallen in love with became this awful gasping corpse who used to be my man.

He wasn't killed immediately. He was hit head-on by a semitrailer truck on a switchback on Highway 1. He wasn't killed when his car was thrown off the road and tumbled down a boulder-strewn ravine and landed on the switch-backed roadway below. He wasn't killed when he smashed into the lower road and was struck a second time by a Jeep.

What killed him, finally, was me.

He lived for nearly a year on a feeding tube and a respirator. With his eyes closed, his brain permanently logged off. And finally I asked a night nurse if she would please turn off his respirator for a few minutes. Just long enough. Long enough to give him his peace.

She was a big, matronly woman named Chile. I guess it was a nickname, I don't know. Chile and I had become friendly. And when I finally worked up the nerve, she didn't say a word. Didn't react. Just nodded. In a real serious, real sober way.

"Why don't you go home, get some rest," she said.

I gave the corpse a kiss. And I sat out in the parking lot and I cried. I cried until my eyes went dry and just ached. My whole body ached and felt like a fist that could never unclench. What else was there to do? I was his angel of death.

The next morning, I got a call from the nursing supervisor at the Ukiah hospital letting me know that Simon Ambrose Rosensinski, my dear, dear companion and best friend, had taken another left turn on the Yellow Brick Road and was headed off some place I couldn't follow.

So I was lonely for a long time. Feeling like a doll whose seams had burst and all the stuffing had come out.

And I was angry at a God I no longer believed in.

For a long time I lived in a fog. Didn't eat, didn't think, and didn't feel.

I lived off of savings, and the only person I saw—the only person in the world—was Peggy. She had her own crosses to bear.

She'd lost her boy Sam. Little Sammy Boy, Peggy's youngest, was born with multiple, multiple birth defects. He was mostly blind, and he had spina bifida. He was mentally challenged, or whatever they call that now. And he had heart problems. Peggy had him in her early forties. He wasn't supposed to live more than a year. But then he reached his first birthday, then his second and third. And we all breathed a sigh of relief. He was a sweet soul. Put on this earth to pour out love.

Sometimes Rose and I would take Sammy Boy out to the beach and help him build lopsided sand castles and things. He loved the feel of the wet sand, and he loved the sun. He would lift up his face and strain his neck like he was trying to come unstuck from his twisted up little body and fly into the sun.

When Sam was almost nine, his heart got the better of him. It started out as an increasingly irregular heart rhythm, and then it just gave out.

At his funeral Peggy leaned her face against mine, her tears running and running down my cheeks. "He was too beautiful," she whispered to me. Hardly able to speak. "Too beautiful for a world like this."

Terror firma.

Poor Peggy was just unmanageable in her grief. Just unmanageable.

Her husband, Skip, couldn't take it. Skip skipped. He headed off to Oregon to work for the park service up there, and we never really saw him much after that. He would send presents to Marc and Brenda Ann at Christmas.

So Peggy had her grief, and I had mine. Two gals headed into middle age with hearts that felt like anchors.

Then one day I realized I didn't feel anything at all. It kind of sneaked up on me. Something went click in my brain. And I woke up about four years later, and I was ready to live this life. I actually felt lighter, like someone put helium in my bloodstream. Eager to get out of bed in the morning. Ready to run my own business and to be a part of life in Green Ash. Ready to make new friends and be a part of my extended family.

Got back to the office that afternoon and called over to Brenda Ann and Peggy's house. Wanted to check in with Brenda Ann and let her know she'd gotten her wires crossed. Again.

The phone rang and rang, and finally the scratchy recording came on. It's Brenda Ann's voice: "Not here, leave a message."

And I wait for the beep. After I get the beep, I say, "Peggy, pick up the phone."

About twenty seconds go by.

"Peggy, it's your own sister. I know you're there. Brenda Ann, you there?"

Another few seconds.

"If one of you girls don't pick up, I'm coming over. You know you don't want that. Come on, Peg!"

Finally, the machine cuts me off. And I mutter some unpleasantries under my breath.

Peggy, Brenda Ann, and little Brady live in the beautiful old Victorian I'd grown up in with Mama and Poppie. Peggy was my older sister by nine years. She'd inherited the place by virtue of the fact that Mama kept a very unscientific tally and came to believe that Peggy went to church more often than I did.

She got the house, and I got the boot.

The house was situated back off the road a little way. The cyprus and the eucalyptus trees crowded in close on each side of the narrow drive, leaves and branches slapping at the side of the windshield, the shadowy little road made a gentle left turn and then—tah-dah— you entered a wide, grassy clearing, and there's the house, white as bone, tall and austere, prim as a prairie bustle. A wide, dark porch wrapped three-quarters of the way around. The deep-set porch windows showed only the yellowing lace curtains inside.

The upper half of the house was sided in what looked like the skin of a white reptile. Those shingletype things, some kind of French style. A single tall window peered at the approaching visitor, and just above that both sides of the roof met at a steep pitch.

"Hello, beautiful," I always said to the house.

If this were thirty-five or forty years ago, I might have seen Poppie coming around one of the corners of the house toting a toolbox. A straw Bing Crosby hat pulled down to his eyes, a big, fat grin on his face. His pants would hang loose all around him, and they'd be held up by skinny black suspenders over his white T-shirt.

On the porch I might have seen Mamma on tiptoe using a broom to wap at cobwebs overhead. And my ailing, gentle-giant, crabby grandfather sitting in an old Adirondac rocker looking at, but not really reading, Reader's Digest.

If this were six years ago, over there at the picnic table, there would be my Rose. He'd wave and pull his black-rimmed glasses off and rub the lenses on his shirt. He'd keep talking to the others gathered around and laughing while he did it. He would rub the lenses briskly

I'm sorry for making you think like that + I'll try not to make you do that ne more.

Thank-you for letting go to Amy's + for letting me stay longer

♥ Jacquie ♥

Your Welcome
I just want u to grow
in God. I
I love U

mom.

Chapter 2

and then finally look down at his glasses as if to say, "Are you quite finished?" Then he'd put them back on. It was such an automatic motion.

I see other men do it—Dan Hanson had done it in his office doorway—and I wanted Rose back. I wanted him back with his nerdy, black-rimmed glasses. I wanted him back.

This is now. It's always now. And no one is outside, and the windows are closed even on a nice spring day like this. The grass already needs to be mowed, and the cobwebs, once I'm up on the porch, are thick and white in the corners. Much of the porch floor is hidden under a damp layer of leaves from last year. Some tree branches have even blown in, a few nestle around the old Adirondac chair that's bleached and split and should either be thrown out or completely remade.

I knocked on the door and without waiting tried to open it up— normally it was open. This time it was locked. Some part of my brain wanted to pretend it was just stuck, so there I was shoving against the door, rattling the handle, and calling out my sister's name.

I knew she was there. She never left.

For a time after Sam's death she would leave the house to go to church, but now the local cable channel, Channel 45, carried the weekly service live on television. That's the last time she went anywhere. Brenda Ann runs all the errands and, in general, plays hotel manager in exchange for rent.

I hollered for a while, and then stomped around the back, where I grabbed the little wooden handle on the screen door and practically pulled the whole thing out of the door frame. It was just clinging to the frame by one bent nail in the top hinge.

"Peggy!" I bellowed.

Snorting steam and pawing the ground with my hooves, I bull-moosed my way through the laundry room. Nothing but filth. There were little drifts of crusty blue laundry powder in the corners of the cement floor and ratty women's underthings draped over lines strung haphazardly all over the room. Half-empty boxes of Tide were jammed between the washer and drier. Squashed and stepped-on shoes everywhere. I waded through smelly heaps of dirty clothes.

The kitchen was not much better. Unwashed silverware was all over. Plates and mugs piled in the sink. Blackened banana skins slopped over the sides of the uncovered trash can. The place stank of mold and old dishwater.

"What happened to the dishwasher I gave you girls?" I shouted to the universe.

A slight raspy peep-of-a-sound came from the other room.

"What?" I called out.

Again there came an answering sighing, uneven pip-pip peep of a voice. And I stormed into the 'great room.' It wasn't looking so great. Newspapers here and there, stacks of needlepoint magazines, and scraps of fabric.

The fire crackling and snapping away in the fireplace was odd, given how nice and springy it was outside, but at least it was cheerful and drove a little of the gloom from the house.

"It broke," Peggy was saying in a weirdly high-pitched voice. Almost the voice of her childhood. Like she was acting out the part of a child.

She was seated in one of those wing chairs looking like Old Mother Hubbard with an afghan across her lap and her glasses pushed up into her hair. She had a large coffee-table book in her hands, and she was slowly turning pages. She hardly bothered to look at me.

"It broke? The dishwasher broke?"

"It stopped working," she repeated.

"Did you call Sears? It's still under warranty. I'm pretty sure they'll come out and fix the thing. That kitchen's a nightmare, Peg. Did you call Sears?"

She hemmed and hawed and finally said, "I don't know if the phone still works."

"Well, it rang about ten minutes ago. I called."

"I didn't hear it," she said in her whispy voice.

"Didn't-hear-it my foot. Are you completely crazy out here? I've never seen the place in such a state. Look, look at this," I went to one corner of the room and pointed up at the ceiling. "Look at the cobwebs here. And your curtains, look at the beautiful old curtains."

I went and shook the lace curtain and a pound of dust must have come unstuck, filling the air around my head. I coughed and waved my hands to disperse the cloud.

"You are living like a crazy woman," I said. "I may have to call the health department. This place is a hazard to human life."

"What?" she inquired after a moment. Still not paying much attention to my arrival. It'd been almost a month since my last visit.

"I said, you're living like a crazy woman. Am I gonna have to haul your tired old person out to the nut farm?"

Chapter 2

A sour, disappointed look twitched across her face. "You sound like Marc."

"Marc," I muttered.

"He said something to me. You know words have power. About neuroses. Being crazy. Maybe it's just his way."

"What?" None of that made sense to me. "What are you trying to say? I know you're trying to say something." Then I'd had enough, and I headed back through the door. "Oh, I can't stand it. Come into the kitchen. I can't stand the thought of all those nasty, rotten dishes."

I huffed into the kitchen and fiddled with the knobs and things on the face of the dishwasher and got absolutely no response. So I straightened up and decided to attack the sink load of dishes head on, tipping each of the plates and bowls sideways and draining off all the smelly, cloudy, week-old water. Then got the hot water steaming out of the tap, located a bottle of Palmolive, and got to work on the dishes.

Meantime, Little Miss Spooky Woman followed me in and perched on a chair by the little table. It was a place where the sun spilled through the window and lighted up her hair in a way that made me gasp. My own sister—her hair was almost snow white.

"You've stopped coloring your hair," I announced.

She nodded. "I just got tired of it. I think my natural color is fine."

"Sure it's fine," I said. "It's just kind of a shock."

"What's the point with all that other fuss?" she said, referring to the hours she used to spend hunched over the upstairs bathroom sink with little vials of Stinky Dye # 15 and whatnot.

"So what were you saying about Marc?" I asked.

"He was here awhile ago, you know, and he came in and took one look at this place and, I don't know ... maybe my crazy-lady hair ... he made up his mind about something, I guess. He just looked at me funny, like he felt sorry for me, but also a little, I don't know ..."

"Disgusted?"

"Um. Maybe. Maybe, yes. I don't know. But he said I had neuroses. And he—you know how he says things. Like he is so sure of what he says, you're tempted almost to believe him. You know? When someone says something with such conviction, you're a little bowled over by it. Overtaken by it. Well, so I went to a book and I looked it up, you know. I looked up neuroses. And I started to read it, and it sounded very negative. Over all. Very scary and sad emotional problems. But then something wonderful happened."

"What?" I rinsed a plate and looked over at her and saw a beautiful smile on her face.

"Well, I put the book down, and I prayed a little prayer. I said, 'Lord, I'm a little afraid of this. What if Marc's right about me? What if I am a little crazy?' " she laughed in an embarrassed way. "I said, 'You have to show me how to understand this, 'cause I'm not a big smart person, I'm just me.' "

"Oh, Peg."

"No, it's true. You eventually have to face facts about yourself. I'm not a big, smart person. So I waited a little while, and then I picked the book up again, and guess what was the first thing I saw?"

"I'm not going to guess."

"You couldn't guess."

"I'm not gonna try, just tell me."

"Well," Peg said, "I picked the book up when I felt brave again. The mental health book. And the first thing I saw was the word neuroses. Except this time I saw it in a different way. Oh, it was wonderful, Mer, because it came at the end of a line and they'd had to split the word. They'd had to hyphenate it. Words have such power. They'd had to hyphenate it, and so what I saw was neu and roses. You see? Neu, it's the French word for—"

"New roses. Right."

"I have new roses."

"You have what?"

"You see it, don't you? There's nothing to be afraid of. God always takes away one thing, but he always gives you something new in its place. So if something has happened to my mind, Mer, it's because there's something new and wonderful waiting for me. God took away my old roses and has given me new ones."

My arms came out of the warm, sudsy dishwater, and I wiped myself off with a little towel. I looked at her. "God took away your son and your husband and to compensate for that, he turned you into a wacko. Is that it?"

"Don't say that."

"Yes, but that's what you're saying to me, Peg. You're saying that God took away your son and your husband and now the fact that you're a nut case is all part of some divine plan?"

"I know you understand me," she said. "I know you understand what I'm saying, you just . . ."

Chapter 2

"I don't understand!"

"You're combative by nature."

"I'm not combative," I said combatively.

"New roses," she said, smiling in a way I could not altercate with. "See? It's like winter and spring. It's like the seasons. Nature is God's other book. In winter all the old roses die, but then spring comes. And then we get the new roses."

She meant it. This thought had strummed her heartstrings somehow, and she was singing its heavenly tune.

I turned back to the dishes.

"Are you saying that you now have God's permission to be crazy?"

Her reply was firm. "Merideth, I'm not crazy. And I'm not sliding downhill. I'm just seeing things in a new way. My mind is open to things."

"What things?"

"Eternal things. Things that are eternal."

"Can't you open your mind and do the dishes at the same time?"

A gasp. "Don't be like that. Nobody likes a smart aleck," Peg said.

"I'm serious, Peg. When I'm at home," I said, "and I do my dishes or scrub my shower or one of those type things, those are the times I do my best thinking. I'm not being a smart aleck. I'm just saying that enlightenment and a clean kitchen can go hand in hand. You don't have to take up one and forget about the other."

She was silent for a while. Agreeing to disagree, her face turned to the afternoon light.

"I'm not ruining the house, you know," she said. "It's going to be all right."

"I know what you're getting at, just drop it," I said, grunting, picking at a hard glob on the bottom of a frying pan.

"This house will be yours again someday, and you can keep it in any way you like."

"This is your house, Peggy. Why would I want your house?"

"Because you love it, because it really is part yours, and I've been horrible and selfish about it."

"You are a crazy 'indaviddle,' and you should seek medical attention," I said, preoccupied.

"I know, I know," she said, giving up trying to have that conversation again for the 10,000th time.

"You can't pawn this old place off on me," I said.

27

My pager went off just then. I pulled it out of my pocket and read the number. I grumbled to myself. It was one of those inspectors out at the old schoolhouse.

"I thank God I don't live your life," Peggy murmured.

The pager went off again.

"And I thank whoever that I don't live yours," I retorted. It was Bernard Hunt calling. Why? Why did I have to get mixed up with people like him? Why was he such a nutball? Why was everyone so off their rockers?

I pulled the plug and let the sink drain.

"I have to go. Tell Brenda Ann I talked with her teacher. Have her give me a call."

Peggy smiled. "She got you out there then."

"Yeah, to talk to her teacher about something. She's got to learn that not everyone is out to drive a stake through her heart." A pause. "What do you mean got me out there?"

Peg gave a little laugh. "Brenda Ann thinks her teacher is quite a dish."

"A what?"

"You know her."

"Pul-eeze. She's nowhere near his age!"

"No, he's more your age, isn't he?" Peg said.

"Oh, at least," I answered.

Peggy gave me a goodbye wave and went to the other room, saying over her shoulder, "I'll tell her to call you."

For reasons I couldn't explain, I felt the blood coming to my face. "I think you should."

CHAPTER
3

Driving back into town, my mind was all jumbled up. Poor Peggy was slip-sliding away. I could feel it. I could feel some kind of rope sliding through my fingers. In a daydream I imagined her at the far end of that rope just floating off into the unknown. It was like being in that old religious painting with me standing on the slick ball of earth, and my own sister floating away into outer space, into the starry night, no longer subject to the laws of gravity. She was a balloon person, her little brain filled with helium or something. What could I do?

On the other hand, I was thinking about this Dan Hanson fellow with his lanky good looks and his fuddled-up hair. And Brenda Ann. Had she set that meeting up on purpose? Did she want her old widow-woman aunt to meet that stargazer for some reason?

I felt a silly grin work its way up to my face, and I tried to make it go away. I was in town now, on Main Street. There were other cars around, people in crosswalks. I didn't want to be driving around town with a silly looking grin. It's not good for business.

I parked around back in a small, sunny lot I shared with the employees of the Green Ash Gift Emporium and the 24-Hour Nautilus. Inside, I turned the sign on the door and checked the phone messages. Something like ten or fifteen messages, one from Cindy over at the Chamber of Commerce reminding me about a donation I'd promised to some charity group or other. Another from American Express getting after me for being four-and-a-half minutes late on the payment of my corporate credit card. Can you believe those people? Other odds and ends.

I got a number off my pager and called Vernon Reece, who was out inspecting that old schoolhouse on the Pompidou property. I wanted to get all the loose ends on this property deal tied up so I could get Bernard Hunt, ESQ, out of my hair.

Vernon answered his cellular phone out at the site.

"Hi Vernon, it's Merideth Dill," I said. "Got your page."

"Yeah, Merideth. I was poking around out here at the old school and came across some stuff you oughta take a gander at."

"What kinda stuff?"

"Well, I'm not sure exactly what it all is. And I think you might wanna keep it quiet. You know? Don't wanna scare anybody off. Wouldn't want the newspaper to get a hold of this."

"The newspaper, for Pete's sake. What're you getting at?"

"I'm just saying," he said, laughing in a nervous, weird kind of way. "I'm just saying, that's all."

"You're not saying much."

"A person might think twice about buying a place like this. That's all."

"Well, Vernon, I just got in, and I've got a pile of stuff to catch up on. Can this wait? I mean ..."

I checked the clock on my desk. It was a little after 3:30. The day was getting away from me. It's times like this I wish I had a receptionist or something.

"Listen," I said to him, "how long're you gonna be out there?"

"I have some paperwork I can fill out," he said. "I can be out here another twenty or so."

"All right, I gotta get someone to watch the office. I'll be out soon as I can."

"See yuh then."

"Yep."

I flipped through my Rolodex and came up with Brenda Ann's pager number. Maybe she wouldn't mind making a little extra money.

I called her pager and hung up. Straightened up my desk, started pulling a file—

Phone rang. It was Brenda Ann. I explained my problem. Turns out she was out at the college in the Spanish lab.

"Can you come over and watch things?"

"Yeah, you gotta give me a minute."

"Make it quick. We have things to discuss," I said.

I thought I heard some kind of laughter from her end as I was hanging up. Why would I want a Dan Hanson in my life? Why would she think that?

By the time Brenda Ann got herself to the office, it was just after four. The day was shot, and I was feeling pretty unstrung. I called Vernon, and he said he'd stick around if I was really coming out.

Then Brenda Ann decided she needed to get a taste of the exotic and glamorous world of real estate and tag along.

"No," I said.

"Look, I won't even be here an hour, nobody's gonna call now anyway," Brenda Ann said. "Why don't I just go out there with you? Maybe I could learn something. You know, about property rights or ... I don't know. Whatever you do. Real estate stuff."

"I need someone to watch the fort," I said.

"Come on," she whined and wheedled and cajoled. "How am I ever gonna get myself a career of some kind if I just sit here answering the phone?"

"Answering phones is a respectable career."

"Oh, right—and why aren't you a receptionist, *hmm?*"

"OK, OK, OK." I sighed and put my hand to my head. "Where's Brady?"

"I dropped him off with Mom."

"No wonder it took you half an hour to get here!"

"Well ..." she shrugged without apology.

How I disliked her at that moment. "All right, but you have to remember, when I call and say I need someone to watch the fort, that's what I need. I don't need a junior partner. OK? Got that?"

"Yeah, I got it. It's just that I'm gonna sit here for forty-five minutes doing a whole lotta nothing. I mean, come on, I need career guidance."

"You want guidance?"

"Here we go," she rolled her eyes.

"Take that unholy ring out of your nose," I said. "There. You've been guided."

"Come on," she moaned.

"You can think I'm old-fashioned, and you can think I'm over the hill and all the rest, but listen to me, sweet sister—"

Brenda Ann snorted and laughed.

I smirked against my will. I pointed a finger at her. "Listen now. You will never become a member of the Chamber of Commerce with that thing in your snout."

"Yeah, OK. Whatever."

I grumbled loudly as we headed out back into the thin afternoon sunlight. Some clouds were coming in off the ocean. I locked the back door, and we hopped into the car.

I was scooting around the back of a logging truck and taking the road out of town.

"I saw your teacher today," I said.

"Really." A note of hilarity in her voice. She was facing away from me, but I could see her smirk in the side mirror.

"Yeah, you're right. He's a real jerk," I said soberly.

She turned to me, crestfallen. "You think?"

I nodded my head, frowning. "It's a shame someone like that becomes a teacher, you know? Out there guiding young minds. What you want is someone who's thoughtful and . . . concerned for the good of others. Really puts some whoo-haa into learning. Some friendly zip and zing, you know?"

"So did you guys talk?" A creeping uncertainty, "Or . . . what happened?"

"We talked. Oh, we talked, all right. He actually said he could give anyone he wants a report to do. You know, acting like this little ruler of the universe. I-can-do-whatever-I-want kind of attitude."

"He did?" Stunned.

"Oh, and the real clincher, the real clincher—you'll like this. He wanted me to call him 'professor.'"

"No way!"

I shook my head to convey all kinds of things that had to do with disappointment.

"No way! Nobody calls him professor. That's . . . I can't . . . are you kidding?" She gave a hoping-for-the-best semismile. "You're joking."

"I am not joking. I wish I were joking. For your sake, I wish I were joking. What an old fuddy-duddy he is. What an old swampy, boggy old fuddy-duddy."

We were moving up into a heavily wooded hilly area. The two-lane road doubled in on itself, making a sharp leftward turn, and I slowed the car, geared down, and glanced over quickly to see Brenda Ann staring forward, eyebrows tucked together, puzzled. Filled with disbelief.

"He is quite good-looking, though," I admitted.

She stared at me. There was a moment of don't-mess-with-me, followed almost instantly with a spreading smile. "You did like him," she cried.

"He seems OK," I said.

"I can't believe you. You are so full of it. I can't believe you. He didn't make you call him 'professor.'"

I shook my head. "No."

"And he wasn't really a swampy, stupid old whatever—whatever. Right? I mean he was really nice, I'll bet. I'll bet he shook your hand."

"And he read my business card," I said. "And he seemed appropriately impressed."

Now she was all eager and obnoxious. "So whadja really think?"

"What did I think? Brenda Ann, I'm not fourteen! I don't get crushes. I'm not boy crazy. He seems like a nice man. He seems like someone who's trying to help you. That's the important thing. I can't believe that your devious little mind cooked up such an idea. This little meeting."

"He's not married," she said, suppressing a grin for my sake. "I mean, he was married, I think, at one point he was. I don't know the story, but I think it's like you and Uncle Simon. You know? I don't think it's anything weird or evil."

"What do you mean weird or evil?"

"I mean I don't think he left his wife and family or anything like that. It wasn't an affair or a horrible divorce or some gross thing like that. I think maybe he was married to a woman who died."

"But you don't know. You don't really know."

"No," she shook her head. "But that's what I want it to be."

"Ah. That's what you want it to be."

"Yep," she said. "I imagine that Mr. Hanson was married to a beautiful woman with long, flowy hair and stuff, and she had one of those long sort of diseases. But a beautiful one. You know? One of those diseases that last for years, where you lay in a beautiful white bed, kind of propped up by pillows, and people come, and they call on you, and they visit you, and they hold your long, cool, pale fingers and weep silently because you're so beautiful and yet death has its cold, deadly grip on you."

I laughed skeptically. "You only get those sorts of deaths in movies and things."

"I know. But that's what I imagine," she said.

"You think what's happening to your mom is beautiful?"

Her head swiveled toward me. Slowly. An odd, scared, defiant look on her face. "What's wrong with her? There's nothing wrong with her."

"You think?"

"What're you talking about?"

"I'm worried about my sister, Brenda Ann. I was out at the house today."

"Yeah?"

"The place is a mess. It looks like crazy, trashy people live there. No offense, of course," I said to her. "I know you're busy with Braden and school and whatnot. But letting your nest go to pot like that—it's the first sign that you're losing your hold on things. Losing your grip."

She was quiet for a moment. "I should do more."

"No, hon. That's not what I'm saying."

"Thing is, we're both so busy. Like you said."

"How is she busy? How is Peg busy?"

"She's always doing something," Brenda Ann said vaguely.

"I haven't seen her up to much."

"Well, how is that your business?" She laughed and gave an off-kilter smile that too soon vanished. "You're not there much. I mean, you come by, but what do you really know about what Mom's up to these days?"

"I'm just saying."

"You come by one day out of the month and—what? Some clothes are on the floor? Maybe we haven't vacuumed in the last two hours?"

"It wasn't just that. It wasn't . . ." I stumbled. "It was the way she was talking too. I mean, it was spooky stuff."

"She's lonely. You know? She's lonely. Her arthritis in her hands isn't getting any better. She can't play the piano much or do her needlework stuff. The dishwasher is busted. She's headed toward senior citizenhood with a whole lotta nothing in her life. You know? There's me—the big disappointment to everyone. And there's Marc down in L.A. And that house. That's all she's got to show for herself.

"Brenda Ann . . ."

Bitterness and tears were choking her voice. "She doesn't have a husband. She doesn't have one of those happy-happy, joy-joy families. You know, like she should have. Like she deserves. People like you make me so mad! Talking about her like that, like there's something wrong with her."

That got me. "People like me? I'm her sister. We grew up together. It's OK that I'm concerned about my own sister. It really is OK. That's part of being a family, you know."

"I know," in a small voice, wiping at her nose ring.

"She hasn't left the house in years."

"I know."

"I know what she deserves," I said as gently as possible. "I know what would make her happy, and you're right—she doesn't have all those things that she grew up expecting to have. But she's got you—that's not the disappointment you think it is. And she's got Brady Boy. That's her joy now. That little guy."

Brenda Ann laughed and wiped at her red eyes.

"None of us have what we expected to have," I said. "It's all changed."

"Did she talk about her new roses?" she asked me.

"Yeah."

"It's her way of coping with things."

"I suppose it is."

We drove in silence for a mile or so. The dense forest of pine and redwoods slipped past the window. The increasing fog and clouds turned the sky a low white mass of dirty cotton.

"Where we going?" Brenda Ann asked.

"I got a property out here that's in escrow. This lawyer in San Francisco wants to buy the place, but before everything is finalized, a whole bunch of reports have to be done on the property."

"Like what? What kinda reports?"

"Well, water quality is one. You have a guy come out and take a water sample, and he runs it through the lab, and they run out a report—lists all the stuff in the water. Hopefully, it turns out clean."

"Is that what we're going out for?"

"No...no, I got some spooky call from Vernon Reece, he's the guy who comes out and evaluates structures. This property has an old schoolhouse on it—"

"An old schoolhouse?" she asked, a mild tone of recognition in her voice.

"Yeah, it's called the Pompidou property; has a nice ocean view. Real pretty."

"I think I know about it," she said.

"You know it?"

"Oh, yeah," with uneasy significance.

"Have you been out here before?"

"No," she shook her head vigorously. "I've heard about it. Kids go out there and fool around."

That was troubling somehow. The way she said it. "What do you mean? Like smoking the funny stuff?"

"Yeah, that and . . ."

"What?"

She was being evasive. I waited.

"Well," she shifted in her seat. "There's just stories, you know? Stories of . . . I don't know."

I shook my head and decided I had no more patience for this. "Well, it's just an old schoolhouse. The only thing that worries me—and if you wanna get into this game, you should pay attention. The only thing you have to worry about is this: We got this old schoolhouse that's been condemned by the county. So you can't live in it, can't use it at all, unless you sink some money into really fixing it up. New foundation, new roof, new electrical, new this, new that. On the other hand, you probably can't tear it down either. My guess is that the county historical people would raise a fuss and haul your person off to court."

Brenda Ann fidgeted, leaning forward and picking her thumbnail at the heater vent. Click . . . click . . . click . . . click . . . and she would sigh, short blasts from her nose.

"What is it, hon?" I asked.

"Nothing . . . I feel funny about going out here. I guess that's stupid."

"What's bugging you?" I said.

"I've just heard stuff, like . . . like they made some movie out there. Some scary movie and someone, I guess, died while they were making it. And, like, there was this old woman who lived out here . . ."

"Yeah . . ." I said, trying to draw her out, trying to get at why any of this was disturbing.

"I don't know . . . dumb stuff . . . stuff we used to talk about in middle school. You know at slumber parties, stuff like that."

She went on with her nervousness, and we came to a little

broken-down gate off the road, and we bounced and heaved through yawning potholes in the old dirt road. The road circled around a hill, and rocks popped and pinged in the undercarriage of the car. Finally we came to an open space in the trees: a wide, wide grassy space that had a grand view of hills and farther off, the white fog blanket over the ocean. On a clear day, it had a perfect view.

Even in this hazy overcast it had a distant, lonely, romantic feeling. And the schoolhouse, to look at it from the outside, did not seem all that decrepit. It was literally a one-room schoolhouse in the old-fashioned pioneer sense. It was mostly stone, which is probably why it appeared to be in such good shape.

It was very simple in design, dark gray, rough stone walls—some of the old whitewash still covering parts of it. Tall six-paned windows set in along the sides. Much of the glass was missing or broken, and you could easily see the sky through the windows on the far side. I stopped the car and got out and meandered around the front of the place. At the peak of the roof, over the entrance, was a bell tower. Just a little squat steeple-looking thing.

The roof sagged in the center, and it looked like an old gray dragonhide that was missing lots of scales.

Vernon Reece's truck was parked on the far side of the building, and he waved and finished eating a pear or some piece of fruit. Wiped his hands on his pants and shook my hand.

He was a short, thick man with round glasses, a baseball cap pulled tight on his head, and thick black sideburns. He had thick, rubbery-looking skin like a baked apple. Could have been somewhere between fifty and seventy.

I introduced Brenda Ann, whose shoulders were folding in on themselves from the cold, and she smiled in a small, unfamiliar way and gave his hand a quick squeeze.

"This is some place," I said, breathing in the air.

"Yep," Vernon said. "Sure is. It sure is. My great-granddaddy went to school here way back."

"Really?" I exclaimed. Fascinated.

We were standing at the steps that led up inside. I was shivering a little myself with the evening coolness. Wishing I'd brought a jacket.

"Yeah, there used to be a little town, a little mining town, I guess, over that way," he said, gesturing in the direction of the ocean. "And this was the school."

"Wasn't it called Hell Town or something like that?" Brenda Ann said in a fast, chattery voice.

Vernon turned to her and gave a look of "you nuts?" "No," he said with a chuckle as he looked to me. "No, it was...I don't know, it was some name. But it wudn't Hell Town. I can tell you that. That's just ..." waving one arm. "One a those rumors that gets going . . . you know how that is . . . it wudn't Hell Town, though." He shook his head.

"So what're we looking at here?" I clapped my hands together and looked to old Vernon. I guessed he was the type to stand around jawing about this, that, and the other all day. I needed to put the pedal to the metal, here. I had stuff to do.

"Well, it's really none o' my business, you understand," he said, taking careful steps up to the doorway. "Watch yer step there."

"How's the flooring?" I asked when we peered into the dark hull inside.

"It's sound enough," he said. "You won't likely fall through."

I looked to Brenda Ann, who had a grim, determined expression. I began immediately to see why we had been called out.

"You can see what we're looking at," he said dryly, pointing to the far wall. As a group, we walked up the center of the room. There were none of the old desks, but the floor was littered with rocks and pieces of split wood ripped from the walls, chunks of plaster, a crumpled sock, cigarette butts, squashed beer cans. Dust everywhere.

Against the far wall, recessed into the back, was a small stage-type area. Against the plaster on the wall were markings of smoke and foul words. In the center of the wall there was a large circle with a star in its middle.

I'd seen this kind of thing before somewhere, and it seemed as though someone puffed cold breath on the back of my neck. I dared not turn around, however. I shivered and pretended it was from the cold. I wrapped my arms around myself for comfort as much as for warmth. This circle thing, it sent a panicky feeling, startled-lamb sort of feeling all through me. I wanted to run.

"What's that?" I asked Brenda Ann, nodding toward the wall.

"It's a pentagram," she said.

"What's that? I mean, what's it supposed to mean?"

Vernon shrugged. "It's a devil sign of a sort." He turned to Brenda Ann. "Right? Some kinda thing..."

Chapter 3

She shook her head and blinked. She was scared. "It's evil, it . . ." Her breathing was heavier, quicker. "It's like an opening that allows in evil spirits and stuff."

On the stage lay an old blue-and-white striped mattress. I worked up my courage and climbed up on the stage and saw that there was a hole ripped in the center, a hole about the size of a person's head, a place where bits and blobs of off-white fluff stuck out. The whole thing was stained in dark, hardened blobs.

"Oh, my," I said, a hand going to my mouth. I swallowed against a thickness in my throat. "Oh, my, this is awful. This is blood." I turned to Vernon and then to Brenda Ann. "This is dried blood!"

Vernon bent into a little heap of feathers and rocks and weird odds and ends, tiny white bones, and he held up a little dark, shriveled thing. Like a small dried fig.

"This is a body part of something," he said.

Brenda Ann made a strangled, swallowing noise and made her way to the door, holding her sleeve to her face.

"You all right?" I called after her.

She just batted at me and was gone.

"What is that?" I asked Vernon, looking back at the thing in his fingers.

He shook his head, dropped it. "Part of some critter. Probably a chicken."

"What is this?" I gestured to the blood and the trashy mattress and the devil sign on the wall. "You ever do this when you were a kid?"

He bit the inside of one cheek and glanced slowly around. "Nope." He kicked at a beer can.

I was overcome. I seemed to sense a presence. An unkind, mocking, inhuman force. Maybe those pentagram things really worked, I thought.

I wanted to laugh all this off as bored Green Ash teenagers getting their kicks, but it seemed serious.

I thought of that lawyer and his twenty-eight-year-old girlfriend on a yacht in Half Moon Bay. What would they say, how would they react, knowing that some kind of grungy altar to the underworld had been built on their dream-home property?

Quietly to Vernon I said, "What do I do here?"

"Clean it up," he said. He sniffed. The cold was bringing on mucus. "I'd bring in a couple trash bags, sweep this up, I can take the mattress if you want. Get that outta here." He looked at the pentagram. It had been painted in blood, we could both see that now. He went up and tested the plaster with his fingernail. A large piece flaked away without much effort.

"That'll come down pretty easy," he muttered.

"Don't think the police should check this out? They investigate this kind of stuff these days."

Vernon worked his mouth one way, then another, gazing down at the floor.

"You wanna sell this place, right?" he said and smiled. His teeth looked strange to me. There seemed to be too many of them. A little puff of white was coming out of his mouth.

I nodded.

"I wouldn't call 'em," he said. "What's the crime here? Place is condemned. They bring a chicken out here, light some candles . . ." he shrugged. "Kill a chicken in a slaughterhouse, that's OK. Kill it out here, it's a crime?" he chuckled. "It don't make no sense either way. 'Specially if you're the chicken." Suddenly he seemed to me like a quiet, sour man who probably didn't have a wife at home. "It's a funny world, you know. Funny world." He smiled sadly. "Stupid, no-good kids."

He waited a moment, his mouth hanging open, for me to come up with a remark that agreed with that sentiment. He waited, and when it didn't happen, he sort of shrugged and hopped off the stage. He tugged at the mattress, and I grabbed the other end. Together we lugged the fetid, rotting thing to his truck and tossed it in the back. A great cloud of dust and feathers choked the air.

"I sure appreciate your letting me know about this," I said.

"Sure thing, like I said, it wudn't none of my business, just a professional courtesy," he answered. He climbed into his truck, started the engine, turned on the lights, and slowly made his way down the hill on that rutted dirt road.

I gave a loud sigh. A great big exhale, trying to push the tension out of my body. I hate being scared of anything. Makes me mad. So I was trying to get a grip on myself. Back in the car Brenda Ann was rigid, sitting forward, both hands holding onto the edge of the dashboard.

I started up the car and turned on the heater. The warm air coming out of the vents felt soothing. Easing away the cold that felt so unnatural somehow.

"I want to get out of here," Brenda Ann said. Her eyes refused to look in the direction of the schoolhouse. "Can we go? Please?"

Her mouth sheered upward, grimacing, and her voice was girlish and tearful. "Please? Come on."

"Honey," I soothed.

I got the car going.

Brenda Ann sniffed and rubbed her nose on her sleeve. "I don't ever want to go back there, OK?"

"Sure, sure."

"Why'd you bring me here?"

"Brenda Ann . . ."

"Stop the car, please."

"What?"

"Stop the car, please," she said, sniffing hard. She sat forward for a moment when I slowed down and stopped. Her hands were on her face, her hair pitched forward.

I rubbed her shoulder. Her body was shivering. I kept the engine running so the heater would help bring her around.

"I wanna pray or something," she said between her hands.

"Yeah?"

"Yeah, will you pray? Please . . ." she brushed back her hair and looked at me through her wet eyes with fierce intensity. In a quiet, quiet beseeching voice, "Please, would you?"

I said "sure," and we held hands, and I said a few words to God. I wasn't sure what to say. More than anything, I was afraid for Brenda Ann. I'd never seen her like this. I prayed for peace. When I said "Amen," she squeezed my hand.

Brenda Ann was quieter, and she said next to nothing the whole way back, but I could tell that the more distance we put between us and that old schoolhouse, the more relaxed she became.

By the time I dropped her off at the office, she smiled weakly and said, "Maybe I don't so much want to become a real estate agent."

We got out of the car, and she leaned against the hood. That little walled parking lot behind the office was quiet. A little music drifted in from the 24-Hour Nautilus next door, but it was peaceful. Night was coming on, and the street light overhead was beginning to flicker.

"You all right?" I asked.

"I guess," she nodded. Caught her breath.

"I'm sorry about that stuff up at the Pompidou property. That's some sorry business. I—believe me—I never would've taken you up there if I'da known any of that was waiting for us."

"I know," she said. "And I shouldn't get so shaken up. That's just dumb high school kids and . . ." she hesitated.

"What?"

"It's just that . . ." she crossed her arms and held them close to her chest. "You know that semester I went up to Humbolt State?"

"Yeah."

"Well, one of the reasons I wasn't in school there very long was 'cause some of the people I ended up hanging out with. I mean, it started off really casual and everything. Just—there was this guy Donavan, and he was really into all this devil-pentagram stuff. And I shouldn't have done it, but I hung out a few times and . . . This Donavan guy, he could . . . like . . . know what you were thinking. I swear. And he could make blood come out of his eyes."

"Oh, Brenda Ann!"

"I know." Apologetically.

"You saw this?" I asked.

"I swear I saw it. I mean, Aunt Merideth, that stuff is real. I'm here to tell you. It's real. I mean, I'm not a real churchgoer type, but I have seen stuff. Real scary stuff, and I know that there is Good and there is Evil. It's out there."

I gave her a hug. We talked a little more after that, but sometimes you have an experience, and you don't really want to talk about it a whole lot. You don't want to be with other people for a while. You want to go off on your own and think about it and digest it for a while.

That night I had a dream that I've never been able to fully remember. Or to forget. Just flashes of fear. Images of running. Running down a long, twisted passageway. Like on a spaceship or something. Running from something. Some swift, horrible presence. Somehow in that weird logic of dreams, it made sense that Dan Hanson and I were in this dark maze of tunnels. We're running from this dream-thing that maybe had claws, maybe had flapping leathery wings. Finally after half-remembered falls, getting caught in barbed wire, and swimming through black glue and too many close calls to count, we come to the end of the tunnel, a dead end, and there's a huge pentagram. A hideous living thing. It seemed to communicate somehow. And even though we're caught between one kind of evil behind us and another evil here before us, I say to Dan Hanson, "We have to jump through this. It's an opening. We have to go through this pentagram!" And I could tell that there were people on the other side. I could tell that the land of the dead was on the other side. But Dan wouldn't go through. He'd rather get eaten by the thing chasing us than jump through the pentagram.

It was my last dream before waking, so when my eyes opened, it was all still with me. This awful cartoon-of-a-dream. I woke up and wanted him there. I wanted Dan Hanson there. And because I was still half-awake and half-asleep, I almost called him.

After I showered and started making toast, I suddenly felt so foolish.

CHAPTER
4

A few days later, I set aside an afternoon, and I put on my work clothes, took my gardening gloves, and drove back up to that old schoolhouse. It was a vastly different sort of day. The sun was high and brilliant in the sky, and when I rounded the hilltop and emerged from the trees, there in the middle of a wide pasture of springtime grass sat that little stone schoolhouse. The wind combed through the green, green grass, sending waves and ripples of sunlight through the field. Beyond the grass, though, and beyond the school was the ocean. No fog today, no haze. Just a picture of the diamond blue sea stretching out forever and ever. I just had to stop the car and try to take it all in. So beautiful. So overwhelmingly beautiful it almost made my brain hurt.

Seems like we get so accustomed to ugliness and mediocrity that when we see a scene like this, we can't take it in. There's something inside us that refuses to take it in. It's a survival technique, I suppose. If we really acknowledge such divine beauty, really love it, and leap into it with all fours, then nearly everything else in our workaday lives—ironing an old blouse, sharpening pencils, calling the post office to complain about service, flipping through the dimwitted stuff on TV, fiddling with pilot lights—would be drained of what little happiness might be in them.

My Poppie said once that we get little glimpses of heaven, just to remind us. God's little Post-it notes, I guess. Reminding us that there's something better.

Chapter 4

I drove down the little graveled lane to the schoolhouse, got out and tied a bandanna around my head, and slipped into gardening gloves. Then I opened up the back and pulled out my leaf rake, a handful of black plastic garbage bags, and a broom.

Armed with gardening tools, I was ready to do battle with the forces of darkness.

I pushed through the creaky doors and peeked inside. This time I was struck by the sense of serenity inside. Of quiet and of history. I could picture little rows of pioneer school desks with their inkwells and their slates. Little boys wearing broadcloth trousers and little girls in bonnets.

Sure, the floor was dirty and cluttered, and wind whistled through broken glass in the windows, but there was nothing here to fear. Nothing.

Pools of bright light dotted the floor here and there. The breeze kept the dust stirred up, and shafts of golden light beamed downward from holes in the roof.

At the stage area, I took time to examine the garbage our little devil worshipers had left behind. Pieces of some poor chicken. Feet and feathers and other grim bits and bobs. Stubby black candles had melted to the stage floor. I used the handle of the rake to dislodge one and threw it in one of the garbage bags.

What would make someone do this? I wondered.

Curiosity? Anger?

Maybe it was something else ... As I picked through the beer cans and the condoms and razor blades, I tried to picture what would have to happen in a kid's heart to bring themselves to something like this.

That's when I heard a noise. Made my heart stop.

I looked up. Tires and rocks. It was coming from outside.

I went to the window, and my soul shriveled up inside me. It was one of those fancy sports utility vehicles. One of those earth-toned "off-road'" vehicles for people who never went off a road in their lives.

I knew who it was.

Shoot, it was time to get professional.

I spanked the dust off my dungarees and headed outside. The sun was blazing, and I shaded my eyes. The vehicle stopped, and a man stepped out on the driver's side. A much younger woman was applying lipstick inside. Making her preparations for getting out.

Bernard Hunt was a pretty big guy, large rib cage, large head full of prematurely white hair clipped neatly to his skull. He was wearing expensive-looking outdoor wear. A fishing-type vest that didn't have a single lure in it. Neat, clean forest-green jeans and unscuffed hiking boots.

I removed one of my gloves, and we shook hands.

"We were in the area," he said, "and thought we'd stop by to remind ourselves why we're going to all the trouble."

"You picked a nice day for it," I said.

He agreed in a sober, intense way. It wasn't hot, but beads of sweat were beginning to stand out on the balding forward part of his head.

Mr. Hunt's girlfriend appeared now, lipstick perfect. She was a pretty, very thin, serious, short-haired young woman. Her outfit basically matched his. I imagined these folk had a professional shopper at Nordstrom in San Francisco. They told their professional shopper they needed outfits for getting backwoodsy.

She shook my hand, and it felt damp and slightly acidic. She started to say something; then her cell phone trilled, and she smiled one of those oops-there's-my-cell-phone smiles, and wandered a few feet away, speaking quietly, earnestly.

"Just wondering what roadblocks are standing in the way today," he said, looking at me in a slightly amused way, like I was a minor character in a movie about rural yokels and yahoos. Like he expected me to whip out a banjo at any minute.

"All the reports should be finished by next Monday or Tuesday— I'll fax everything down to you then," I said, and gave a slight shrug. "That should do it."

"What about this place?" he said, nodding to the schoolhouse. Before I could respond, he twisted around to his girlfriend. "Carmen— what about this? Huh?" He made a bad-smell face. She made a bad-smell face back and shook her head. "Nah."

Bernard Hunt turned back to me. "I mean, it's condemned anyway, right?"

"Right—what'd you have in mind?"

His shoulders gave a flicker. "Take it down, you know. It's about where I'd like to see the tennis courts." He looked past the schoolhouse with the air of gazing into the future. His future. His big, landowner future.

Chapter 4

"I envision the main house over here," he said. "It's gonna be kind of a French Morroccan design. It'll have kind of a stucco finish, and it'll be stressed, you know? Stressed. That'll give it a seventeenth century villa sort of a feel, right? Like a Louis XIV kind of a deal."

"And the tennis courts here," I said, nodding at the schoolhouse.

"Right. Then . . ." He turned and with a grand, visionary sweep of his hands toward the ocean, "Then a pathway, right? Kind of gardeny thing and a pool there, pointing to a small knoll some fifty feet in the distance. So when you're in the pool, you're lying there, right? And your view will go straight from the pool right over there into the ocean."

"Uh-huh." All of this was supposed to be really impressive. It only succeeded in annoying me.

"Then," he continued, "over thataway, I don't know, a guesthouse and maybe another pool." He swiveled around to the girlfriend. "Carmen—whaddya think? Guesthouse needs a pool?"

She shook her head in the affirmative.

He retraced his steps. "So pool, guesthouse," turning back toward the oceans, "Pool, gardeny-pathy thing," sweeping back up the way he'd come. "Main house, then here—boom—tennis courts." He looked at me squarely. "'Course, all of this depends on you. Getting us through the paperwork jungle, making sure we're not gonna get ramrodded somehow. Right?"

There was the urge in me to punch him. "Well," I said, "I don't know about your knocking-the-schoolhouse-down idea. The local historical people might come after you."

"What do you mean, come after me?" he asked. His fists went to his sides. His head cocked. Looking for a fight.

"Well, it could be considered by some to, you know, be a historical landmark."

"It can't be a historical landmark," he fumed. "It's just been sitting out here going to pot. Place is falling apart. All this land, this fantastic view, just going to waste." He shook his head and pulled his lips tight. "I've had run-ins with those twerpy little historical people before. You know, just a bunch of tea drinkers. Librarians who never got married. Twerps. Twerps is all they are."

Carmen turned suddenly. "Hey, David needs to talk to you about that cash thing. You know, that loan—"

"Yeah," Bernard Hunt snapped. "Yeah, fine."

He trundled over to her like a bear that had been stung too many times trying to get his honey. He grabbed the phone. "Yeah, hey David . . ."

The girlfriend picked her way toward the entrance of the school-house. She was very young, young doelike eyes, creamy smooth skin.

"Creepy old place," she said. "Looks like something from a horror movie."

"Really? You think? I kinda like the old place."

"I just wanna peek inside and—"

"It's awfully dirty in there," I said.

"I just wanna see it before we tear it down," she said, moving toward the stairs.

"It's a condemned building. County condemned the place years ago," I said, "If anything happens to you in there—it's an enter-at-your-own-risk type deal."

She cast a suspicious look my way. She wasn't stupid, she knew I was trying to talk her out of going in.

"I just want a look around," she snapped. Then smiled.

She pried open the doors, and I just let her go in. Wasn't anything else to do.

In a moment I heard a slight exclamation, and I poked my head in, "You OK?"

Her eyes were blazing! Her arms stiff at her sides. Sick and scared.

"I had a feeling about this place," she said. "When we drove up, I told Bernie I had a feeling."

She brushed past me into the brilliant sunlight. Then she turned and gave me a look of reproach.

"I was trying to just clean up in there," I explained.

"Did you do that? Is that what people do here?"

"Me?" That came out of nowhere. "No," I laughed.

Her body lurched a little when I laughed. I guess I don't realize how loud I am sometimes.

"I was just cleaning up," I said. "Shoot no, I haven't the foggiest who did all that. The guy who was up here doing the structural report called me up here a few days ago. I didn't have any idea 'til then. It kinda shook me up at first, but I figure it's just some kids."

She still viewed me with suspicion.

"It's about ready to fall down, anyway," she said. "We'll just tear it down. . . . I guess that's what we'll do . . . although . . ." She sighed loudly and looked over at Bernard Hunt gabbing away angrily with the David person on the other end.

She approached me carefully. "The truth is, Bernie really doesn't have the money for this place," she smiled. "He just wants things. You know?" She gave a tinkling little laugh. "He always gets them one way or another. By hook or by crook, like he says. But I don't know about this one. I don't know."

I felt an uncomfortable stirring in my guts. "Well, he better know. He's going to be signing the papers in a few days."

"Oh," she rolled her big eyes. "He'll pull a cat out of the bag or whatever. He'll do it—I just can't see how."

"Are you a lawyer too?" I asked her.

"No," she said, getting serious. "No, I study art."

"Really."

"I used to study science. But now I study art."

"What sort of science? Like biology or . . ."

She looked at me like I'd belched. "I studied science," she said. "Science."

"But now you study art."

"Right, I have a tutor."

There was something strangely robotic about this young woman.

When Bernard Hunt got off the phone, she dragged him inside, and I heard more exclamations and other noises of dissatisfaction. He was talking loudly, and I just tried not to listen. This was a strange pair of folk, and I just wanted to sell them the place. And then "sayonara."

Mr. Hunt emerged from the schoolhouse coughing and choking like he'd just come out of a burning building. The girlfriend followed.

"That's an outrage," he said.

"I agree," I said calmly.

"You know who did that in there?"

"No, I don't."

"What were you doing in there? There're rakes and things. Trash bags."

"I was just—"

"You were just! You were just what? Just misrepresenting this place?"

"I was cleaning it out, Mr. Hunt."

"There's a fine line between cleaning up and misrepresentation as defined by law," he bellowed.

49

"What if this place is cursed?" the girlfriend said, her thin little eyebrows creeping toward each other.

"What?" Mr. Hunt looked at her with annoyance. "Oh, get a hold of yourself."

"Well, I mean, who believes in that kind of stuff?" She said. "But still—you see things about haunted houses all the time. Ghosts and poltergeists."

"If you're planning on tearing the old place down," I reasoned, "then I don't see the harm in my cleaning out some chicken feathers and whatnot."

"This is no case of chicken feathers," he said, poking his wiener-dog finger at my face. "This is something of a different stripe. You know what I mean. This is something of a different stripe altogether."

"This isn't chicken feathers," she agreed, shaking her head.

"This is most definitely not chicken feathers," he agreed soberly.

They were in agreement on this point.

They continued to agree that something wasn't right, and they got back into their off-road vehicle, and they bumped and jostled back up the lane and disappeared around the bend back into the woods.

I went back inside and finished my clean-up job. It was dusty, dirty work. Prying up the black candle wax. Scraping the plaster where the pentagram was painted. My mind was going and going, thinking about those two. I figured that they had decided not to buy the Pompidou property. He didn't have the money. They were nervous—nervous about the devil stuff. And why not?

I needed a strategy for getting this thing into the hands of another buyer. Nothing on my list was selling. It was weird. Other realtors were selling places like mad. But me—things were slow.

An insurance payment was due—my broker's insurance. You lose your insurance, you're out on the street. You don't mess around with insurance.

My rent on the office space was due. My phone bill was around $400 bucks, late about two months.

Nonetheless, when all the reports were completed a few days later, I faxed them to Mr. Bernard Hunt's office, and soon afterward the escrow office informed me that the sale had been completed, and I received my much-needed commission of 5.5 percent.

It would not be the last time, though, that I would have a run-in with Bernard Hunt. Next time would be serious. Next time would be the crash.

CHAPTER
5

Almost a week later, I pulled my aging body out of bed. Oh, boy. My back was sore in three places, and my head felt funny, and my nose was all stuffed up. I'm not crazy about mornings to begin with, but I get through them. I drank a glass of water with my eyes closed. Did my shower thing and my breakfast thing and my putting-on-clothes thing.

If I were to advertise myself in the real estate circular, here's what it'd be:

> Fixer-upper's dream—Looking for a project that'll bring
> lifetime reward? Here she is: Seen better years. Broken
> pipes and drains, bats in the belfry, sits on spreading
> acreage. Life's not been kind to this property, but with a
> little spit and polish, she'll be the warm, happy hearth
> you'll be proud to come home to.

I took some pills for my water retention. Scrape, scrape, went my slippers on the kitchen linoleum. Zoop, zoop, they went on the ribbed plastic hall liner. Somewhere along the line, my nose came unclogged. That was nice. Breathing is nice.

About that time I realized my arm hurt. Shoot. I didn't have time for that.

When the arm hurts, it's going to rain. Sure as banks.

I rubbed the sore place with a little Ben-Gay.

"Now you really smell like an old lady," I said to my reflection in the bathroom mirror.

Chapter 5

To double-check the signal from my arm, I put my glasses on and peeked out the window above the sink and up into the pale sky—yup—there were long lacy strips of clouds flipped up at one end. Called cirrus clouds. I remember that because Rose told me they looked like the tails of white circus horses. And they do.

Cirrus clouds nearly always mean rain. So that was that.

Out of the cupboard came a big, plastic mixing bowl that I placed on my small dining-room table. To call the room a "dining room" was being grandiose. The table and all kinds of other junk sat at one end of the rectangular room and the couch, TV, and bookshelf, and even more junk—hereafter known as "living room"—were at the other.

It was not a large condo. If it were mine to advertise, I'd have called it "cozy." Cozy always means cramped.

I put the bowl on the table and then eyeballed an irregular orange stain on the cottage-cheese ceiling. By adjusting the bowl's position a millimeter here and there, I was satisfied that when the rain began and the roof started to leak, the water would drip-drip-drip directly and steadily into the mixing bowl.

Then out of the linen closet came three towels that I rolled tightly and pressed into various windowsills that allowed rain inside.

OK, truth. I lived in an awfully cramped, awfully overcrowded, little condo. Alone. Oh, did that ever strike me that morning. Here I was plummeting into the far side of middle age. No kids, no husband, no real home.

Not to complain. I always threw myself into what life I had—kept the place spotlessly clean. Almost sterile. Constantly going around the place flicking the feather duster.

I would sew new covers for the throw pillows on the couch every year. I would buy a small chair at an estate sale or rescue a beautiful old rug from a flea market.

Books of all shapes and colors and widths crowded the bookshelves.

My closets were stacked and packed with vibrating foot soakers, orthopedic devices to help alleviate muscle strain in necks and spines, various water piks, blood-pressure monitors, and other medical things purchased over a home shopping channel.

Photos of family and friends crowded the walls. Each room had five lamps where one would suffice.

Ferns and minipalms and fresh-cut flowers occupied corners,

upper shelves, everywhere. To watch TV I had to pull back drapes of Wandering Jew.

But sometimes feathering your little nest isn't enough.

You can shop in all the stores from sea to shining sea and still never find that thing you really need.

That missing inner piece.

On top of the TV was a picture of Rose and me. Sitting in a pretty little frame among the plants.

The picture was taken just before the accident. He'd decided he needed to learn how to play the clarinet. And he went to Green Ash Community College and plunked down his money, and a music teacher named Yolanda something-or-other taught him the basics.

So there's this picture of Rose in a short-sleeved shirt blowing into his squeaky, squawky clarinet over in Peggy's living room. He's standing up, proud as a pumpkin, thinking he's Benny Goodman, and I'm sitting in a chair to his right, grinning. For some reason, I was wearing his clunky, black-rimmed glasses. One of those funny things that happens on a Saturday night. Someone snapped a picture of it.

I picked up the picture and—as I always did—gave it a kiss. A silly thing to do, but I'm a silly indaviddle.

New roses, I thought, looking at the photo. I had to think along those lines now, didn't I. I had to think about new roses. New . . . but I didn't want anything new, anyone new. I wanted him back. Why couldn't I have held on to him? Why did God let me fall in love with a man who was going to get killed?

I wanted that picture to come to life. I wanted to press my fingers into my ears as he honked away on that stupid clarinet. I always told him he was going to attract love-starved Canada Geese with that thing.

Right after the picture was taken, he had plopped down on my lap, and I probably protested, acting like he was gonna break me in two.

What I wouldn't give now. To feel that weight crushing me.

By the time I got to the office, the sky was already darkening. Just after ten o'clock, hailstones the size of grapes came pouring out of the heavens. Bouncing and Ping-Ponging on impact with the street and the roofs of parked cars. After a few fantastic moments, the hail let up and rain poured down in buckets. People dashed past the front windows, covering their heads with newspapers, pulling their jack-

Chapter 5

ets up as hoods. Excited tourists began emerging from the Green Ash Gift Emporium tugging price tags off new umbrellas.

I stood at the front window, gazing up at the downpour. Across the street at the trendy little coffee/espresso shop, the windows were filled with teenage faces staring happily into the sky.

A German tourist couple burst through the front doorway, wiping rain off their faces, smiling and nodding to me, and gesturing, wanting to search through my photo book of listings. Pretending interest in the local real estate market. Once the rain let up a little, they waved in a friendly way and headed toward a cafe.

I was feeling blue. That sense of loneliness that first set in at home hadn't gone away. The rain didn't help. What started as a cloudburst eventually settled into a steady, drizzly shower.

I had prepared a lunch for myself, and it was in the refrigerator in back. How I wanted to be going to a small cafe, meeting friends, cracking jokes, catching up on things . . .

Around noon, I turned the sign on the front door and feeling weary and waterlogged and sorry for myself, slumped into the back. I pulled the meek little brown bag out of the refrigerator, and out of the meek little brown bag I withdrew my meek little pickle sandwich.

At home, the fridge had been a little bare, and I had to get creative with pickles and a few pieces of rye bread, a jar of horseradish, and other odds and ends.

I sniffed the sandwich. The bread smelled like the refrigerator.

I sat on a plastic milk crate and turned on the TV.

There on Channel 9 was old what's-his-name daubing paint onto a canvas. I'll call him Jim, this guy who does this painting show on the local PBS channel. He's got long, real neat straight hair, pulled back, and he's a little on the chunky side. His voice is amazing. So hypnotizing.

A voice that sounds wise. Gentle. Sounds as if it knows the answer to things.

Today his paintbrush gently stroked the canvass, and as he spoke in that voice like tiny bubbles breaking and wind shushing through tall grass, I was taken away. Thinking thoughts about men I hadn't allowed into my head for a long, long time.

Remembering what it felt like to run the palm of my hand across a face that needed a shave. That scruffy, scraggy, rough sensation. What it was like to walk along a street holding a big muscly hand.

Nowhere special, just a street. Not Rome or Paris, just out in the middle of the afternoon walking with my hand in a hand like that.

The painter turned toward me, smiling, making some point about brush strokes. When he smiled, Jim had two slightly prominent front teeth. They stuck out just a little bit. So when he smiled, so friendly, so very proud of his work, he looked like a big old buck-toothed hamster.

He was so cute, I laughed out loud with some tears in my eyes.

For some reason, that did it. I looked down at my half-gnawed-on sandwich and a jumble of leftovers and decided that even if I had to eat alone, I was going to one of Green Ash's nice little lunch places.

I'd just gotten that commission on the Pompidou property, I had money. I was a successful single gal. What was I doing eating a pickle sandwich in the storage room of my office?

I stuffed everything back into the refrigerator. Such a feeling of giddiness and expectation came over me. It's almost worth getting into a rut for all the joy when you eventually climb out of it.

I grabbed an umbrella, found my wad of keys. Even started whistling a little tune. Out of the closet I pulled my long plastic rain jacket. Brenda Ann gave me so much grief for that coat. It was a purply, semitransparent thing. Just a thing you wear when it rains. I wasn't trying to be a fashion model. Brenda Ann said it looked as if I were wearing a shower curtain.

At the front door, up went the umbrella. I turned to lock up.

"Are you closing up?" asked a voice.

Startled me. I looked ...

Dan Hanson.

Of all people, it was that Dan Hanson. Looking tall and lanky and lean. His hair plastered down to the very bone of his wet skull. A handsome, uncertain grin on his face.

Such a feeling of welcome and warmth spread across my face, like a blush.

"Well, I gotta ..." I started. "A girl's gotta eat," I said. "What-were-uh, were you?" Then I just stopped and made dry spitting sounds. Trying to get these stupid words out.

He laughed.

"How're you?" I said, restarting, smiling, reaching out and grasping his hand. "I was closing for lunch, but if you want to check out some listings ... that's no problem. I have Polaroids."

"I couldn't do that," he said. "I was just down here and ..." He smiled.

His mouth opened awkwardly, and he looked in one direction, then another. He looked in my direction again. "I'm renting right now," he said finally. "I rent."

"Oh," I said, nodding. Smiling encouragingly. "Lots of people rent."

"Yeah. Yes, they do," he said. "When you teach, like I do, sometimes you can't let things get too permanent. You know? I might only be here for a few years."

"Oh, you might be surprised though," I said. "Sometimes buying is just the thing. I don't mean putting down roots. Necessarily. I mean it's smart money."

"To buy a place?"

"Oh, sure. Sure! I know a young couple who bought a house here, oh, about two years ago, I suppose. Nice two bedroom place up on Claremont. You know where that is?"

"No," he said in his quiet, sandy voice.

"It's up off Saw Mill Road . . . doesn't matter. These kids bought the place, and really fixed it up. Ripped out all the old paneling, painted, painted, painted. Put in a whole new kitchen . . . skylights . . . little garden. You know. Two years later, she gets a yen to go study something in Minnesota. Wants to get her master's degree in—I don't know—underwater basket weaving. Well, wouldn't you know it, they list the house with me and bam, we sell that thing, and they made money! They made real money, if you know what I mean."

"Wow."

"So I guess what I'm saying, bottom line—I'm a bottom line kinda gal. I don't know if you knew that."

"I think I did."

"Good. Well, bottom line. You buy a place, it's an investment. You think you might be here two years?"

His head began bobbing in a perhaps-sure-maybe sort of way.

"You gotta be here at least two years," I reasoned. "Anything less'd look bad on your résumé. Right?"

"Right. You're right."

"So now—see what you're doing?" I pointed down to dirty water running in the gutter along the wet sidewalk. "See that? See all that water?" I then pointed out the storm drain twenty feet down. "All that water pouring down into that hole? That's what you're doing with your rent money. You're pouring that money down a hole. Try buying. Seriously. Put your mind to it."

"Do you own or rent?" he asked.

I looked at him long enough to blink two or three times. "Have you eaten lunch?"

"No," he said.

"I started to eat a pickle sandwich in there," I said, nodding toward the office. "I started to eat a pickle sandwich with horseradish on old, stale rye bread. I do own my place, Dan Hanson. But I eat left-overs, and I work eighty-five hours a week. So I guess owning isn't everything. Would you like to have lunch with me? I was going to go by myself. But if you're available for lunch, I think that would be lots of fun. I think that would be dandy."

He nodded in a very serious way; then a long, funny smile came to his face. And he kind of looked at me out of the corner of his eye. He wasn't trying to be cute, he was just unsure about something.

"Yeah, I could eat," he said.

"Good."

I hoisted my umbrella, and we crowded beneath it, and I introduced him to this little Mexican place called "Tres Hombres."

The restaurant was rich with the smells of onions sizzling on the stove, fresh salsa and spices I didn't know the names of. He ordered a plate of nachos, and I had a burrito of some sort.

We sat at a little table under a large painting of General Zapata, and by the time the food came, I decided I liked Dan Hanson very much. We were just shooting the breeze. He was not a big talker, had a soft voice, and I imagined he'd been a shy kid in school.

I asked him what brought him to Green Ash.

"A job," he began. Teaching jobs in junior colleges are tough to get. For every opening, there are 300 applicants. He'd been unhappy teaching down in San Diego. Too many houses, too many cars on the road, too many lanes in the road, too many guns, too many un-happy, hapless lives all crowding in around him.

When he heard of the opening here in Green Ash, he'd applied right away. He'd gone through three interviews and was finally told it had come down to him and one other applicant.

A few days later, a phone call came that he hadn't gotten the job. Then about a week before the school year began, he got another call asking if he could begin immediately.

The other candidate had been accepted into a Ph.D. program at the University of Chicago.

"It's not too swift coming in as a second choice, I bet," I said.

He shook his head. "I guess I don't think of it that way," he said. "No?"

"Not at all. No, that other person had something else she was supposed to do; this is what I was supposed to do."

"Destiny," I said.

"Something like that. I don't so much believe in coincidence. But destiny . . . sure."

I munched thoughtfully on my burrito. All that stuff Brenda Ann had been yakking about was coming back to me about Dan Hanson's imaginary wife dying of an imaginary illness.

"So I have to ask—are you married or anything?"

He took a sip of his drink from the glass. "Why do you have to ask?"

"It's the first thing people wanna know," I said.

"Really." Not so impressed.

"What'sa matter?"

He looked troubled.

"What people want to hear . . ." he started. "Generally what they want to hear is something simple. 'Yes, I'm married.' 'No, I'm single.' 'No, I'm divorced.' Like when you go to the doctor's office, they always ask you to fill out a form and for some reason you always have to check a box that applies to your marital status. As though that has something to do with your ingrown toenail or your persistent cough. Anyway, it's those check-box categories—that's what people want to hear. But . . ." he paused, "But when it's something other than that, then that's what people don't want to hear. When it's complicated. When it's outside the check-box."

"Are you telling me to mind my own beeswax?"

"No, I'm only trying to explain what I've learned on this particular topic. When someone passes you on the street and they say, 'How're you doing?' They're really just saying hello. How you're doing has nothing to do with it."

"I suppose not."

"So when you say you have to ask me if I'm married, then I'm tempted to think that you're not so interested in my story as you are in putting me in a certain category in your mind."

"What do you mean by that?" I asked, kind of getting my hackles up. He was figuring me as some sort of dummy, I thought.

"I don't want to sound rude, but I have the feeling that being married or not, or divorced or not, could somehow change the tenor of things, of lunch, of . . ."

"Now look," I said, "I know you're a teacher and everything, but you're drowning me in words here. You're drowning me! I just asked you a simple question. And you're right in one part. I mean, if you're married, fine, just say so. I'll sell you a house. But if you're single, I'll sell you a house and after lunch here I might ask you out to dinner."

He laughed. "I'm sorry, I just—"

"Here I was thinking you were the quiet sort."

"I am," he said. "People say I am. Look, I'm sorry. I just get going sometimes. I have soap boxes that I get up on."

"I guess you do."

"I am married." He fixed me with a funny look. "And . . . I am single."

"Wait—"

"You wanted to know."

"Sounds like some kind of fancy footwork."

"Not at all," he insisted. "I am married. But my wife took off. We had been married for several years. And she became more and more concerned that she hadn't seen the world. Obsessed, actually. She didn't know who she was or what she wanted, and one day she was gone. She had gone from living in her parents' house to living in our house and . . . The last I heard from her is that she was in Florida."

"And you haven't divorced?"

"I never felt the need to. I'm not even sure how I'd go about doing it. My car is still in both of our names. How can I sell it without her signature?"

"Was she insane?" I asked. "I'm being blunt here."

"How surprising," he remarked.

I laughed and took a final bite off my plate.

He shook his head. "I don't really know when people are insane or when they aren't insane. It often looks like the same thing to me."

"She's insane," I decided. "I'll just tell you. She's bonkers."

"How can you say that without really knowing me?" he asked. "I might have driven her to it. I might have driven her away."

"A woman knows."

He sighed. "After she left and I knew she wasn't coming back, I wasn't sure what to do with myself. I had the summer off and . . . I went to a place in Washington State, a place on Puget Sound. It's like a monastery for Protestants," he smiled. "I spent about a month there."

"Doing what, may I ask?"

"Gardening. Praying. Looking at the stars. I felt this huge . . . weight . . . inside of me. I didn't know what else to do."

"Did it help?"

He nodded slowly. "Yes, it did."

"How long ago was all this?" I asked.

"Oh . . . it's been about four years ago now."

When lunch ended, the rain was still coming down. Dan Hanson walked back to my office with me. He said goodbye and, as I was unlocking the door, I watched him walk away. Not a bad fellow. I liked him. I liked him quite a lot. And I recalled with some warmth in my face, the dream I'd had running down that tunnel, running up against the pentagram. And how I'd woken up in that frazzled state-of-mind, wanting him there.

We saw each other again a few days later. Had pizza. And several times a week after that.

CHAPTER
6

"So you guys are pretty much dating now," Brenda Ann said.

She'd dropped by my office on a midweek afternoon in April. The sun outside was dazzling off car chrome and the blinding legs of untanned Caucasian tourists who'd just started wearing shorts for the season.

"Dating. We're doing no such thing," I said. "Bah humbug."

I gave the side of the fax machine a good whack. Stupid thing was giving me trouble again.

"Now wait," Brenda Ann said. "Let's back up here. Let's just hit rewind, OK? You guys had lunch a time or two, right?"

"Right," I muttered, shoving the paper tray back into the machine.

"And you've gone out to dinner a few times, and you've been to his house a few times."

"You old nosy warthog," I sputtered. "We stopped by his place for about two whole seconds. We were going down to that Indian restaurant near Goat Rock, and he stopped to get his wallet. He forgot his wallet, and we stopped by his apartment. It's not what you think."

"Did you go inside?"

"Well, sure. Sure I did."

"And what'd you think?" she asked, sidling up to me. "What's his place like?"

I straightened up my back, my vertebrae making a symphonic crackle.

Chapter 6

"Did you hear that? That's what your back sounds like when you get old. Old and rusty."

She was standing there grinning at me, one of those you're-avoiding-the-subject grins.

"Oh, for crying out loud, Brenda Ann!"

"What was his place like?"

I moaned and pitched a fit and threw myself back into the screechy chair behind my desk.

"It's just a bachelor pad. It's pretty dismal, if you ask me. How a person can live like that I'll never know!"

"Smelly? Like tennis-shoe smelly?"

"No, not smelly. Not smelly. Just . . . well you know. When a gal like myself has her own place, it's like a nest. It's pretty, and you fill it with pretty things. But men—bless their little pea-picking hearts—just have a place to crash. It's like they get bonus points for living on less. I don't know."

"Books all over the place . . ." she suggested.

"Sure, astronomy books and papers strewn all over a desk and a TV and an old, old couch that looks like it came over on the May-flower and . . . there isn't a single picture on the wall, no plants, no rugs. Nothing nice. Nothing that says 'home.' It's sad. It made me a little sad to be there. It made me sad that this nice man lives in such a damp little cell. That's what it reminds me of—a cell."

Brenda Ann sure knew how to hit my buttons. I'd been stewing about Dan Hanson's living quarters for a couple weeks. I hadn't said anything at the time. No, that's not true. I guess I had.

We had walked in, it was close to twilight, and he turned on the light, and I let out a little gasp. Plain old drab carpeting on the floor. Colorless linoleum in the tiny kitchen.

No spark of life to the place. No creativity put into it.

"This is how you live?" I'd said.

He opened a drawer in his cluttered desk—his desk was in his living room—and pulled out his wallet.

"Yeah," he'd answered, as though it was perfectly natural for a person to live in a tiny, one-bedroom place with no soul.

"Your office at the college has more pizazz than this place."

He gave me a puzzled, wounded look.

"What do you mean?"

I shrugged. "Looks like a bad motel."

"Oh," is all he said.

Oh.

"You gotta remember, I make my living evaluating living spaces," I said.

"Well, this is home," he said, gesturing feebly. Knowing it did not live up to my standards. "What's wrong?"

"Have you ever thought about a touch of paint or . . . or maybe a potted palm, an aquarium?"

"An aquarium?" he laughed.

"A couple throw pillows."

"It's easy to clean," he mumbled, heading for the door.

Couple of days later, I was at the grocery store, and I picked up a copy of House Beautiful. Real casually I brought it to lunch with me—we went back to the Mexican place—and I laid it on the table.

He saw through me right away.

"What's that for?"

"This? Nothing. I was just looking through it."

"I don't want it," he said.

"You can't have it," I answered, and I picked up my menu. While looking carefully through the enchilada section, I said, "Although, there's a good article on giving your home a new look for spring. Some nice ideas."

"Let me see it," he said, taking the magazine. He flipped through the pages frowning, making occasional *ugh* sounds. After one particular *ugh,* I said, "What? What's so awful?"

He showed me an advertisement in the back for an aquarium video. One of those videos you buy, pop in the VCR, and you have two calm, peaceful hours of fish swimming in a fishbowl. On your TV.

"I have one of those," I said. "I got it off of the home shopping deal on TV."

"I'd hate it."

"You wouldn't hate it if you owned it, if you tried it. I have one, it's great. Relaxes a person."

"I can't believe—you really own one of these?"

"Sure! You'd love it."

"I'd hate it."

So much for trying to introduce old Mr. Stargazer to the finer things.

Chapter 6

Of course, I didn't tell any of this to Brenda Ann. She was already so steamed up about me and Dan Handsome—that was her nickname for him, Dan Handsome—I didn't dare give any fuel for her fire.

So there she was sniggering and making insinuating remarks. Like I was having some sort of jet-hot romance. Finally I said to her, "Listen, I have lots to do here. You wanna help me out or what?"

She frowned. "Nah, I just stopped by."

"Well, do something," I said. "Check through my mail, something. Anything."

A big stack of letters and packages had come in that morning.

"All right," she muttered.

"I'm gonna get you a bumper sticker that says, 'I'd rather be gossiping.' I saw one over at the gift emporium."

She started idly picking through the mail. "So when are you gonna see him again?"

"I don't know. He's out of town for a few days."

"You miss him?"

"I'm too busy for that," I said.

I was shuffling some things around in the back for a few minutes and then came out front. Made a couple phone calls. Usual stuff.

"Hey, who's Bernard Hunt?" Brenda Ann asked. Holding up an envelope.

I moaned. "That guy. He's the client I sold that property to. You remember, the schoolhouse property."

"He's writing to you," she said, tugging her finger across the back of the envelope, tearing it open.

"What's he want?" I asked absently.

I pulled a file out of my drawer—glanced over the info on a house in town. Little two bedroom house in rough shape. As I glanced through the information on the place, I made mental notes as to which buyers on my 'potential' list might be interested in something in this price range.

I had hit a dry spell that was turning into a severe drought. I'd seen this kind of thing before. You sell nothing for a couple months, and then out of the blue you sell three or four places in a single week. Feast or famine.

But this famine I was in was serious. And all the time I was devoting to Dan Hanson wasn't helping things. The week previous, so he and I could go for dinner, I'd rescheduled with some clients to show

65

a house, and the next day I found out they didn't want to reschedule, because they'd hooked up with another agent, Gemma Nichols, and she'd sold them a cute little cottage place. Gemma swiped those folks right out from under my nose.

Gemma is only a part-time agent these days. She made so much money in the 1980s down in Marin County that she came here to live in semiretirement at the age of forty-five or so.

Gemma Nichols didn't need the sale, the money, or the clients. I did. And I'd meant to call her up and ask her if she'd cool it and give someone else a chance. Sometimes you can call up a colleague and—

"Aunt Merideth . . ."

"What?"

I looked up from the file.

Brenda Ann's face was white, her mouth small, hard, and open. Her eyes were bad news.

"What is it?" I asked, getting up from the chair.

"I don't believe . . ." is all she could say.

"What does it say?" I asked.

She held out the letter. "He's suing you. He wants to back out of the sale."

"What . . . ?"

She shook her head. "He's taking you to court . . ."

"He can't do that, he—" I grabbed the letter. It was on the letterhead from his law office in San Francisco. My eyes scanned the thicket of words. Big attorney words all crammed tightly together. It was all legal gobbledegook, full of "herebys" and "seeking judgments" and "plaintiffs." But the message was clear to me.

"What is it? What's he trying to do?" Brenda Ann asked, watching me sink back down into my chair.

"Well, this is just stupid," I snapped. "He's—" I shot back up and slapped the letter to the desk and then snatched it up again and waved it around in the air.

"This old fruitloop is saying he gets to back out of the sale because of the water quality report."

"What?"

"See, I had . . . this is so asinine . . . I had Byron Toms go out and do a water quality report. Standard thing. By the book. He does these reports all the time. You take a sample of ground water, and you test it. Well, that report came out OK. But this charmer has gone out now, and he's gotten his own guy to come out and do a report, and he says there's traces of a heavy metal in the groundwater that our report doesn't mention. Well, it does mention it at something like four parts per million or something like that. But Bernard Hunt's report says it's a higher percentage than that."

My eyes went back to the letter. "But that's not enough—he says—the suit is not just to back out of the sale. It's also got a punitive deal attached to it."

Brenda Ann was watching me with large eyes. "Punitive—that means he wants money from you?"

My eyes searched through the maze of words on the letter. Disbelief choking me.

"He wants to back out of the sale, which means I'd have to give back my commission and . . . and . . . and on top of that, he's seeking—the gall, the absolute gall—punitive damages. I mean, that's what it looks like. I'll have to run it by my lawyer. I'll have to . . . go see Jonathan about this."

Brenda Ann stood and came toward me, trying to give me a hug. But I broke away.

"I'm sorry," I apologized. My hand went to my forehead. A blazing headache had just hit. "I'm sorry. I just didn't see this coming. This is crazy. This is just craziness. This is insane. Brenda Ann, you have to watch the fort for a while, OK? Aunt Merideth has to go see her attorney. Can you do that? Can you stay here? Watch the walls crumble?"

Brenda Ann followed me to the front door. "You OK?"

"Fine," a smile snapped up to my mouth. "Sure. He wants it rough, I can play rough."

I gave her a little peck on the cheek.

Jonathan Bale, my attorney, looked like a twelve-year-old boy in a school play on how to succeed in business. He had short blond hair, a little curly and out of control. And perfect skin. I knew he was in his thirties and smarter than most, but sometimes I imagined his feet not quite touching the floor behind his desk.

Normally, our meetings were friendly affairs. He would double-check contracts or glance over some tricky tax maneuver of mine. We would chat about his kids or his wife's bed-and-breakfast.

The day I brought in the Bernard Hunt letter, though, all that levity and neighborliness vanished.

With the letter laying on his desk, Jonathan put on his reading glasses and sat straight and rigid, glaring at the thing. As he read it, his hands smoothed it flat to the desk, slowly, over and over again.

When he'd finished with the letter, he examined a copy of my original water quality report, and then he squinted at the report prepared by Bernard Hunt.

I was aware of the blood pumping in my neck.

"Well, he's coming after you, all right," Jonathan said finally, looking not exactly at me. To one side, thinking, thinking.

"It's crazy. I had to bring it by, I mean—I thought you might laugh," I said.

He looked at me. Very seriously. "No," he said. "This Bernard Hunt—have you ever heard of him?"

"No," I said. "I just know he's some hot-shot outta San Francisco. Got more money than sense."

"Merideth, he's someone to contend with. He's . . . he works on the federal level. Has since the late '60s. He's connected. Well-connected. If I'd known you were dealing with Bernard Hunt, I'd have cautioned you not to. Or at least to tread lightly. I mean, really watch your P's and Q's. I wish you'd told me earlier."

I let out a gasp. "Bernard Hunt's just backing out 'cause he doesn't have the money. His little trophy girlfriend told me so. I shoulda . . . I shoulda paid more attention. I shoulda paid more attention . . ."

Jonathan's fingertips silently tapped the polished surface of his desk. "His girlfriend is Carmen Gatehouse—do you read the society section of the San Francisco Chronicle?"

"No," I said in a complaining voice, feeling as though floodwaters were rising up around me.

Jonathan rubbed his face. "Old San Francisco money. The Gatehouses own hotels, they own sections of the wharf, they elect governors and senators."

"Now, Jonathan, you listen to me now. I don't give a tinker's dam who these people are. I don't care. This is America, and there is a justice system, and there are laws and whatnot. You can't tell me just 'cause I'm little-bitty David and he's big-awful Goliath that I don't stand a chance. He's bought the property, he signed the papers, he plunked down his money—and he can't just change his mind."

Jonathan shook his head. "Merideth . . . it happens. I know of a case nearly identical to this that happened down in Napa a few years ago. Don't think Bernard Hunt isn't acutely aware of that. Don't think he hasn't done his research."

"Jonathan, it's a water-quality report! That's it. He's saying he can back out based on that?"

"We're talking breach of contract," Jonathan said. "He's gonna say he bought a piece of property that was characterized one way and it turned out to be something else. He's saying that your report showed clean groundwater, while whoever did his report found traces of a heavy metal in the water."

"Well, then," I gasped, "this is all laid at the feet of the water-quality guy. It's Byron Toms. Byron Toms did the water-quality report. If anything is wrong, it's his deal, isn't it?"

"You're the agent. It's ultimately your responsibility. If Bernard Hunt wants to go after Byron, he can do that as well. It doesn't say anything about that in the letter, though. You know that's the law, Merideth. The whole thing rests on you. He probably doesn't care about Byron. Going after Byron isn't going to help him get out of this contract."

"Wiggle room," I said. "He's looking to worm and wiggle his way out."

"You're going to need another attorney," Jonathan said, taking a small book out of his jacket pocket.

"Can't you represent me?" I asked.

"I can help prepare the case," he said. "But the courtroom isn't my specialty."

"Courtroom? You think this is going to court?" I wailed.

"Do you want to settle?"

"Of course not! Of course I don't want to settle—I've already spent most of my commission!"

"Then you're going to need another attorney. I know several who would be great."

I stared at his desk. I stared into the gloss of that dark, cherry wood for such a long time that I began to see depths that weren't there. Gazing into it like a crystal ball hoping that some answer would come bubbling up out of the abyss.

"Jonathan . . . can I kill him? Can I punch a bullet right square between his eyes . . ."

"Merideth," he said gently. "I can help you. I can."

"But I'm gonna lose, Jonathan. I can see that. It doesn't matter how this thing ends up. If I go to court and win, it'll still bankrupt me. The court costs, the legal fees, it'll empty my pocketbook and my bank account and my credit cards. It'll wipe me off the face of the earth. Everything I've worked for since climbing out of that pit."

I closed my eyes and saw a deep pit in the earth. Me at the bottom of it.

"When Simon died," I said, "when my precious husband died and they buried him . . . it was like they buried me too. It took me four years . . . four years to claw my way out of that grave. And it's taken me all this time to get where I am now . . . And now this . . . It's gonna bankrupt me either way. If I win or if I lose."

"You have your broker's insurance."

"It won't be enough. It . . . I missed my last payment . . . I've had a dry spell . . . I haven't sold anything . . ."

"Merideth, let me give you the name of an attorney who can help you. I know him. He's just the guy—"

"I can't do this right now," I said. I was starting to feel tears running down my chubby cheeks. "I'm sorry, Jonathan. I have every faith in you, every faith, I really do. But we have to do this another time . . . tomorrow, maybe . . ."

"OK," he said kindly. "OK, but we can't put it off long."

"I know," I whispered.

"Call me anytime. I mean that. I'll drop whatever I'm doing."

"Thanks," I said. "I know you will."

CHAPTER
7

Misery does strange things to a person.

After my meeting with Jonathan, I just drove around. Drove around, drove around, until I didn't know where I was. I was lost in my own town. Trees and cars and houses floating past the windows of my car. Nothing was connected, like the whole world was a jigsaw puzzle all jumbled up. Everything looked weird and foreign.

Then I was on Highway 1; then I was off in a redwood forest somewhere, and three or four times I had to pull off the road because I couldn't see. Tears streaming down my face, coughing and crying. Feeling small. And sick. And so alone. So horribly, completely alone.

"Oh, God," is all I could manage to say. "God . . ."

I thought for a moment of finding Dan Hanson—then I remembered he was away until the next week. And then I was glad he was gone. Why would he want me blubbering on his doorstep? Why would anyone?

Eventually I ended up back in Green Ash, my headlights cutting through the growing darkness. My wiper blades on to clear away a shimmering mist falling in slow-motion out of the low, low ceiling of clouds. It seemed as though a cloud bank had fully descended from the heavens and the town was in the core of it.

I parked in front of my office. Brenda Ann had turned out the lights. No one was around, because Green Ash pretty well closes up at 6:00 p.m.

She didn't have keys to the place, so I got out—*brrrrr,* the air was chilly—and tested the doors. They were unlocked, the cowbell over the door went clang, clang in its cheery way when I pushed on the door. I couldn't go inside. I just couldn't bear it. So I got out my wad of keys, shivering against the cold and fumbling with the lock—everything had a cold, slick coating—I managed to secure the door.

Every movement was difficult. Every movement was a fight against the pain.

There was a big jumble of broken glass inside of me. A big tumbleweed-shaped ball of broken glass inside of my body. It had grown inside of me all afternoon and just seemed to get bigger and bigger so that I couldn't control it. It felt like it would pierce my skin and burst right out of me.

I heard some people coming up the sidewalk. They were coming up the sidewalk through the damp air and the darkness, so I made a move back to my car. I had an irrational fear that little points of glass were pressing up against my skin. I thought these folk might see it.

I felt so scared and scary inside I thought the very sight of me would frighten these people. So, like some kind of Frankenstein monster, I hobbled away for cover.

Hiding in the safety of my car, I looked up and I saw that it was Gemma Nichols and two other people—clients of hers, most likely. Here I was knocking myself out for my business and getting nothing but grief and lawsuits for it, working weekends, working ten-, twelve-, and fourteen-hour days, getting nothing but kicked in the teeth. And here was Gemma Nichols, in semiretirement, blithe as a blue-footed booby . . . getting clients left and right.

I glanced up at her. She was dressed casually in slacks and a loose top of some sort. She wasn't even wearing a jacket. You always wear a jacket, generally with a snazzy lapel pin, when you meet clients. They have to know you're a professional. And her hair—it was all in some kind of curly, loose bob. She might as well have been fifteen instead of approaching fifty.

Her whole approach was much, much too causal.

Oh . . . forget it.

Look whose talking, anyway? Look who's feeling like a failure hiding in her car and then look . . . look who's outside striding confidently up the sidewalk practically arm-in-arm with this young couple.

Chapter 7

All these thoughts careened around in my brain, silver balls in a frantic pinball game.

Gemma looked over at me as she spoke to them. There was a momentary connection between us. Something in her face ... sympathy, kindness ... as though she had stepped out of her conversation with her clients for a split second and had acknowledged me. Knew what was happening to me. Saw that bundle of terrible burning-bush of pain inside me.

Somehow I was saved by that look. I don't know how to explain it, but for the moment a coolness seemed to fall over me. Someone had noticed. Someone in my profession, at my stage of life.

I sat in my car thinking, get ahold of yourself, Merideth. Grab hold of something.

Across the street from my office was that trendy little coffee shop, one of the few places that stayed open past six. Inside, I could see teenagers dressed in black, talking to each other, flirting, laughing, or sitting alone glowering into important-looking paperbacks.

Next door was a furniture store, Barry's Rent-to-Own. Barry Knox was an older gent who had lived in Green Ash forever. He was also part owner of the Green Ash Gift Emporium and a video shop just down the street. Real active in the Lions Club and whatnot.

I stared at the front window of that Rent-to-Own furniture store. They were running some kind of "Spring Madness" sale. They had a whole suite of things in the window. Matching desk, lampstands, couch, recliners, ottomans, and a few other odds and ends. A classy-looking painting of ducks swimming among reeds, a little statuette of an English fox hunter. The whole thing looked like a living room out of an English country home.

And a little plan began to hatch in my brain. A little scheme. Something that might pour a bucket of sunshine down in this pit I'd fallen into. Spring madness, indeed.

I drove through town and hooked up to the highway. Highway 1. Out away from town the clouds had cleared, and the moon was out, and it reflected a long white zigzag across the surface of the black ocean.

A few miles later I came to the turnoff, and I bumped and jumbled up the driveway, brushing past the close cypress branches, to Peggy's house.

Our family house.

In the moonlight the big old two-story house almost looked like a big white ship.

I turned off the engine, which had been on for hours, it seemed, cut the lights, and just sat there for a few moments. Feeling the unfamiliar silence. The silence felt like a thing. A substance like an exotic vapor that was coming up out of the earth underneath me. Rising up around the body of the car and sliding in through the open window, through seams in the floor, the heater vents and the radio speakers. And it swirled slowly and invisibly all around. And then it seemed to soak inside of my skin. Only a millimeter or two, but the effect... so nice... the silence cooled my mind and gave focus to my thoughts, helped me to think about the things I actually, desperately wanted at that moment.

Rose, I thought, where are you? If you could see me, you would reach out to me now... I know you would.

Poppie...

Somebody...

I needed help. I needed someone to say it was going to be all right.

"God, help me," I whispered. "All of a sudden I'm not a big, smart person anymore," remembering Peggy's words.

While sitting and staring at the house, I remembered that old painting my great-grandfather had used in his tent revivals. The one that still hung in my Poppie's old study. The painting of the family staring out across a vast, vast distance of outer space, out toward the golden glow of heaven. And between heaven and earth there were millions of angels, like a golden river of angelic beings moving back and forth.

When I was a little girl, my mother told me that everyone had an angel. Peggy had an angel, and Poppie had an angel, and smelly old Floyd Burchard, who lived down the road, had an angel.

I had an angel. A majestic celestial being of light at my side. Always there.

The silence of the evening continued to seep into me. And I stared out the windshield up into the smattering of stars in the night sky.

"I wish I could see you," I said to my angel. "I wish I knew you were here. Really knew it. It would mean everything... please," my mind begged, "... please..."

And for a moment I really believed an angel might appear. I needed that. I needed a miracle.

Chapter 7

Would it kill an angel to appear for just ten seconds? It would require so little effort on his part, and that tiny effort would change my life. Would give me such comfort in the middle of such pain.

I waited. And I hoped some more.

Then I got grouchy and sad, and I got out of the car, shaking off the magical feel of the silent earth. There would be no miracles for me.

Inside the house Brenda Ann gave me a hug and told me that Peggy had gone up to bed. She wasn't feeling well.

I picked up little Braden, his little feet kicking back and forth in the air and gave him a kiss on his slobbery little smile.

Brenda Ann asked me how things had gone with Jonathan, and I just sighed, "Not good, hon."

She didn't have any words for me. Just put her arms around me and gave me a hug. Little Braden made funny, tired sounds from his chair where he'd retired.

"What've you been doing?" she asked me. "I finally had to close the office up, and I didn't have a key."

"I know," I said. "I'm sorry, I just had to get out and breathe some air, you know? I just have to figure this thing out some way."

"Well he can't sue you. I mean . . . that's just not right . . ."

"He can sue me. He is suing me. He's already filed a civil action. That letter was just serving me notice."

"You'll beat it, though, I mean, the thing to do is bring some public notice to this thing. You get enough people behind it, I know some people who can organize a protest just like we did in Frank Riggs's office that time—"

"Brenda Ann, this isn't like saving trees. You know? It doesn't matter how many times you strap yourself to a bulldozer, hon. It won't affect anything. He can sue me, and according to Jonathan, he can even win. It's been done before. Down in Napa."

"Well, that's not right—it all started with that devil stuff out there. That pentagram and all. See how that stuff works? You didn't wanna believe me, but that is cursed ground. Nothing but bad can come from that kinda stuff."

"Oh . . . I think the devil is as strong as you let him be."

"I'm serious."

"I know you're serious."

Braden made deep, sleeping breaths. We watched him for a moment, that little guy.

She picked him up, and he made tiny complaining noises while his eyes were squeezed shut. His head fell to her shoulder.

"Listen, I had an idea tonight," I said to Brenda Ann, following her to Braden's room. I was going to tell her about My Secret Plan that developed in front of the furniture store, and then I thought better of it. She didn't need to know everything going on in my life. And she'd probably try to talk me out of it.

"What?" she asked.

We were heading up the dark stairs to his room, where she laid Braden down in his crib. We stood over him for a moment, listening to him take long, deep breaths.

"What were you saying?" she asked.

"Nothing."

I left her there and went out into the hall and peeked into Peggy's room. She lay on her side in the bed, facing a night stand where the lamp was on low. I approached the bed silently, and on the stand I saw that her small black Bible was open to the book of Revelation.

"... a new heaven and a new earth ..."

These words and others were underlined in red pencil. Made me think of New Roses.

Peggy coughed once in her sleep.

I sat down beside my sister and stroked her whitening hair. She mumbled in her sleep and continued to breathe deeply. There were nine years between us, but in some ways there seemed to be a hundred. (I had been a mistake. A term my mother did not attempt to disguise.)

I tried to picture us all those years ago in this house, when I was a little brat and Peggy was a little lady. I had inherited her dolls, and I played with them in my usual rough-house, take-no-prisoners sort of way—and Mama took them away from me.

I had cried and begged for them back, but my mother was firm. She sat me down on the edge of my bed and let me know that Peggy's dolls were always so nicely arranged in her bedroom. When Peggy had played with them, the dolls were always getting married and having babies and running off on beautiful honeymoons.

When I played with them, the dolls were always fighting, losing tufts of hair, always in danger from unseen beasts.

Still, I had admired Peggy. She was slim and she swam well. And she talked about important subjects with adults at the dinner table, and she had pronounced big words correctly. She read books with-out pictures. And in her way, she had mothered me. On nights when Mama was ill or had been weeping—Mama wept a fair amount and would retire early to bed on these evenings—Peggy would tell me a story and would help me with my prayers. She would lovingly tuck me in at night. In some ways, I became her doll. A precursor to her own children.

I stroked her hair, and Peggy woke up a little bit. She stirred and mumbled something.

"What?" I asked, quietly.

"Say your prayers, honey," she said, in her sleep. I think she was speaking to little Marc or Brenda Ann or even Sam.

"I did," I whispered.

"Did you wash your face?"

"Yes."

"Go to sleep, now."

"Will you tuck me in?" I said, close to her ear.

She made a small, sleepy sound.

"All tucked in . . ."

I smiled and planted a small kiss on her forehead and turned off the light. Now I was the adult, and she was the weary child. I left her there in her peaceful sleep.

Next morning I woke up after a happy dream of some sort. Feel-ing good. One of those exciting dreams about traveling overseas and having all kinds of adventure.

Then I remembered.

My life. Oh, my life.

This is why depressed people sleep so much. In dreams you es-cape so many things.

The black cloud returned, and I went to the office feeling as though everyone in town was looking at me. Thinking, "There goes the loser. She's going to lose her business. She's going to lose her mind and hole up in some tiny apartment for the rest of her life and shut the blinds."

It's exactly what I felt like doing.

There were no calls on the message machine. I had no sales pend-ing. No angel had appeared yet, and God had left me no written in-structions on how to make things better. I had hoped He might drop a note by the office . . . send a fax . . . no such luck.

At one point, just before lunch, I was fed up with being miserable me—I needed a jolt of sunshine in my life, so I took step one in My Secret Plan. I went across the street to Barry's Rent-to Own, and I talked with Barry. Told him of My Secret Plan. He seemed a little reluctant to go along with it but accepted my check happily enough.

Everything was ready. The delivery would be made. The machinery of My Secret Plan was set in motion.

Dan Hanson is going to love this! I thought, smirking to myself. Mr. Dan Hanson was the one who would reap the reward from My Secret Plan.

The next few days were torture, waiting for him to get back into town. Waiting for the phone call.

CHAPTER
8

The following Thursday night I was at my apartment. Still waiting for his call. I looked at the clock every few minutes. I knew Dan Hanson was supposed to get in around 6:00 p.m., and here it was 8. Then 9. Then 10.

In my mind I pictured him arriving back at his little place, opening the door and—

There he would find something completely unexpected.

A new desk in the corner. The brand new desk would match the brand new couch against the wall, as well as the new bookshelves and the new rug. A painting on the wall of a duck swimming among reeds. A new recliner, a new ottoman. A statue of an English fox hunter. An entire matched suite of home furnishings from Barry's Rent-to-Own.

What would he say? Would he be thrilled, would he—

The phone rang.

"I gotta take mom to the hospital."

It was Brenda Ann.

"What?" I said.

"She won't stop coughing. She just coughs and coughs."

"Did you give her some of that cough medicine?"

"Yeah—it's not helping."

"Is she all right?"

"Well, sure. I guess. They'll give her some special HMO cough drops or something. Thing is, can you come get Brady? Can you watch him?"

"Of course, but why don't you drop him off here. It's on your way," I said.

"Yeah, yeah. That's good. I'll be by in just a few."

"You sure Peg's doing OK? It's ten o'clock at night. Are you going to the emergency room?"

"Yeah, I don't want her to cough all night. It'll be OK. It's probably an allergy, with everything blooming, April showers and May flowers. All that junk."

"All right, hon."

I had just hung up the phone when it rang again. Almost immediately.

"Hello," I said.

"Merideth?"

"Yes ..." I said. The voice was funny, I didn't quite recognize it.

"It's Dan."

"Hi, you're back," I said, a willy-nilly nervousness overtaking me. "How was it?"

"Fine, it was fine," he said.

A silence filled the phone line for what seemed like forever.

"Dan?" I said. "Are you OK?"

"Merideth, did you send all this stuff over?"

"Yes," I said. Feeling his disapproval. Feeling his quiet, solemn horror.

"You have to send it back," he said. "I want this all gone, OK?"

"Dan—I thought you'd like it. Didn't you like it? I pictured you coming back and just loving the way your place looked. I've been so worried about the way you lived. It all seemed too bleak to me. I ... well I wanted to help you."

"This is my home," he said and groped awkwardly for words. "This is ... you can't come here and ... do ... this."

Another long silence.

"I know you did this out of ... it came from a good place in your heart," he said.

"Well, of course it did, Dan."

"But I don't want it. This isn't ... I can't have this here ... I feel like I came back to find my house ransacked."

"Dan ..."

Chapter 8

"I don't think you can understand this, but this place belongs to me," he said. "And I don't want to hurt you, but you have to have them take all this stuff away."

"All right," I said. Feeling so small.

"I'll be gone for most of the day tomorrow, I'll be at the college. I would like when I get back to have everything the way it was. I'd like my old things back. I know how you feel about my things, but they're very important to me. That desk belonged to my father."

"All right. I'm sorry, Dan."

"Where're all my things?" there was almost a sob in his voice.

"In storage. I rented a storage space."

"Can you get it all back here?"

"Yes..."

"Thanks."

"Will you call me? Can I see you?" I asked. "When everything's back?"

He hesitated before replying, and I knew his answer. I knew overwhelmingly that I had become an unwelcome intruder in his life. I had crossed some kind of boundary.

"Never mind that," I said, jumping in before he said it. "Please, don't speak," I said. "I'm sorry... I'm sorry, I'll take care of it. I'll take care of it all in the morning. There's nothing that can't be undone. Everything'll get put back."

"Thank you," he answered. "I'm going to hang up now, OK?"

"Dan... please."

"Merideth, I can't talk to you right now."

"OK, but... OK, then... good night," I said.

"Night."

And that was that.

I heard the click on the other end, it sounded like a door closing. Yet another door closing. Another miracle that would not happen. Another angel that would not be appearing.

Had it been such a bad thing? His house looked like a prison cell to me. I was only trying to help.

Oh, Dan. You don't understand... I didn't mean to hurt you, I didn't mean to come on so strong. It did come from a good place inside of me. The best part of me. I have a lot of goodness in me, and I just wanted to help. It made me so happy to do it... it's the best I've felt in days, knowing that your place would look so nice and feel so homey and comfortable. I felt like I was bursting when I went over to Barry's Rent-to-Own and told Barry Knox about My Secret Plan.

I wanted you to be happy, Dan. I wanted to picture you surrounded by nice things.

I put the phone down and went to the kitchen and started washing up the few dishes on the countertop.

I cursed myself. I denounced and trounced myself.

Yes, I wanted to control you and manipulate you. I wanted to storm into your life like a bull elephant in a china shop. I wanted to scare you off and terrify you. "Look out, here comes Merideth Dill, Licensed Real Estate Broker, to refurnish your house, to seize control! Run, run for your life!"

Oh, Dan.

When Brenda Ann arrived at my front doorstep with Brady, she took one look at me. "You all right?"

"I'm an idiot," I said, and I told her what I'd done.

"You can't do that," she said. Her, the kid with the nose ring, telling me to mind my manners.

"There's no fool like an old fool," I said.

She laid Braden out on the couch and straightened out his little sleeper.

"What are you going to do?"

"I'm gonna get his furniture back," I said.

She gave me a hug. "What are we going to do with you?" she said.

"I don't know. Go on, get Peggy taken care of. Is she in the car?"

"Yeah."

"Are you sure she's all right?" I asked.

She nodded. "It's not like she's coughing up blood. She's just coughing, and she can't sleep."

"OK."

"So I gotta go. I'll just slip in and get Brady on our way back."

"OK."

"Are you gonna be all right?" she asked.

"Sure. I'll do a little cleaning, and I'll fall asleep on the couch and . . . it'll be fine. Go on, now."

CHAPTER
9

The next day I went to Barry's Rent-to-Own and made arrangements to undo My Secret Plan. Barry Knox wasn't too pleased, but at an additional fee, he agreed to send his guys over that morning.

"What made you think he was gonna like that?" Barry asked me.

I didn't want to say "it's because everything is falling apart in my life." So I made something up. I don't remember exactly what I said.

Dan Hanson and I did have lunch a few days later, and we even laughed a little.

He said, "At first I thought I'd walked into someone else's apartment by accident, and I actually went back outside and checked the number on the door. Then I thought I was on America's Funniest Home Videos. I kept waiting for someone to jump out of the closet with a video camera or something."

But it wasn't the same old, glowing spirit between us.

I gave him the willies. I was an unpredictable quantity in his life. No, more precisely: I was a wacko. And who needs a wacko?

We ended things on a friendly note, and occasionally I would hear from him. I liked Dan Hanson very much. And I liked myself very little.

If there were to be New Roses in my life, it wasn't going to be him. And I dreaded what (or who) it would be. With Bernard Hunt's civil action running its way through the legal system, I had the feeling that my New Roses were going to be full of thorns.

CHAPTER
10

By June, I was in the fight of my life for my real estate business. It was a tough climb. A real estate agent trades on her reputation, and mine was shot. No two ways about it. The news was out, and I wasn't getting any clients. All the properties that had the 'Merideth Dill' sign out front were being sold by other agencies, and I was getting half-commissions on them.

I remember that day in June I was sitting in my office staring out across the street at Barry's Rent-to-Own. A truck was out front, and Barry's guys were unloading a bunch of furniture out back.

Crazy thoughts were zipping around in my head every which way.

Suddenly it seemed to me that this is a Rent-to-Own world. Except you don't ever get around to actually owning anything. You just rent it all for a while, you plunk down your money and you just hang on to things for a time, and then they just go away.

The front door opened—clang, clang went the cowbell over the door frame.

I looked up, and there was Gemma Nichols looking like Queen of Quite-a-Lot in all her semiretired glory. A silk top and casual slacks, a scarf in her hair; she looked tanned and rested and supremely successful.

I mumbled a salutation, "Hi, Gemma."

"Hi, Merideth. How're you doing?"

Chapter 10

She smiled sadly at me, and I suppose I smiled sadly in return. She was here to share her condolences. That much was clear.

"How 'm I doing? I'm doing great," I lied.

She had a stack of orange fliers in her hand, and she laid one on my desk. "I have something for you."

I picked the thing up. It was an announcement for tryouts for the local Shakespeare Festival. A little theatrical show that had gone on for years in Green Ash. The ad offered the chance for people to come out and audition for parts in the play *Macbeth*.

"If you want me to advertise in the program—" I started to say.

"No, no, no," Gemma said. "I was thinking you might try out for the play. Lots of people do it."

I laughed hollowly and put the flier on my desk. The last person in the world I wanted to talk to was a successful real estate agent. Certainly not Gemma.

And I certainly didn't feel like discussing special little, fru-fru, extracurricular activities that were enjoyed by those in semiretirement.

"I don't think so," I said. "Thanks, though."

Gemma sat down in the chair next to my desk. She held my gaze for a moment. It was a gaze full of friendly sympathy, a gaze full of discomfort and regret. I remembered her looking at me that way that night in my car, when she was with clients and I was hiding after receiving the news of the lawsuit.

"Merideth," she started.

"Gemma, thanks for coming by. I can't do that though. Really. I have a lot of things going on right now. You know."

"I know," she said. "I was really sorry to hear about what's happening with you. You don't have to believe me—the business we're in is very competitive."

"Shark-infested waters," I said.

"Yes, but I'm serious when I say I'm so sorry to hear what you're up against. It's terrible, and it's unfair. And what affects you affects all of us in this rotten little business."

"I suppose it does."

"It could have been me, it could have been any one of us in town," Gemma said. "Why Bernard Hunt chose you? Who knows . . ."

"I just drew the short straw," I said.

"I was just thinking that something like this," she indicated the

Shakespeare flier, "might take you out of yourself for a while."

"Yeah." I had stopped looking at her and was toying with a business card of mine that was lying on the desk.

"You can take this any way you want," she said, "But sometimes the universe does things that look horrible, but they're really just new ways of helping us find freedom and expression."

"The universe?"

She smiled an indulgent smile. "We all have our different words for it. You may call it God. Someone else may call it—I don't know—Buddha. I call it the universe."

"You don't think that sometimes life just stinks?

"One door closes and another opens. Believe me. That's the way the universe works. It may be time for you to stop being in real estate. It may be time for you to do something else."

I looked up at her. "It may be time for me to shoot Bernard Hunt between the eyes."

She laughed. "Well, it might be time for you to be a pistol packin' mama," Gemma said.

I snorted and laughed.

And then it got quiet again.

Then there was a moment of discomfort. Gemma and I didn't really know each other. We were just doing that making-conversation thing.

"Just think about the Shakespeare festival," she said. "You'd be surprised how much fun it is."

"Well, I've never done that kinda stuff in my life."

"Not even in high school? Everybody does this stuff in high school."

"Yeah, I probably did some of that. I don't know. I couldn't get up in front of a bunch of people and spout a bunch of thees and thous, wherefores and 'hark I hear the trumpet blow,' or whatever. However that works."

"It's not that bad. I did it last year, and I was so, so intimidated by it at first. You're right, the language looks real scary on the page. I mean, it was all written 400 years ago. But I have to tell you, it's a lot of fun, and you may not believe it, but it was the best therapy I've ever had."

"What do you mean?"

"It was really freeing," she said with a wide gesture. "It's using your voice and using your body and feeling the energy in the different places inside you." She said all this while squirming around in the chair and moving her arms around in an exercising sort of way.

"You're losing me—we're still talking Shakespeare, right?"

"Yes," she said, a little winded. "Well you know how there are different places in your body where your energy comes from—like golden orbs. Doing the Shakespeare Festival helped with that."

"With what?"

"Finding those golden orbs. Inside me," she said with a radiant smile.

"I don't get what your getting at."

"I'm not explaining it very well. I guess I'm just…" she laughed. "I guess I'm saying that when you're all knotted up inside, there's nothing like getting up on stage and acting like a fool."

I smiled. "Well, now you're talking my language."

"Think it over. I can't encourage you more strongly. I might come by and bug you about it again."

"Don't do that," I said. "I'll decide if I want to do it or not."

She looked a little shocked.

"I'm sorry," I said. "I guess I snap at people. But I just—with everything that's happening. The last thing I need is someone bugging me."

"I can understand that," she said. "And I'm sorry. Really. I just get so enthused about it. And I really can't help but think it might be just what the doctor ordered."

"OK."

She stood to go. "I've been thinking about you a lot, Merideth," she said. "I know I've never come in here before, I mean, I guess we've met a few times at Chamber functions. But it's funny. When I walk by your office, I can feel you. When I drive by here, I can feel you."

Oh boy.

"Uh—" I started. "Well."

"We should get together sometime. Do you like chai?"

"Well," I paused, "Maybe if I knew what it was…"

"Oh, it's tea. Chai is tea."

"I like tea," I said.

"Then you'll like chai," she said. "Like I always say, just give it a chai."

She liked her pun, and she laughed heartily. I swallowed against a clot of acid in my throat.

"Well, thanks for this," I said, holding up the orange flier.

"Think it over—the universe may have something fun in store for you."

She gave a little, fluttery wave of her hand and "clang, clang" went cowbells, and she was off in a blaze of sunlight. She managed to vanish completely into the afternoon glare like a spirit.

It's funny what an idea will do once it's planted in your brain. Gemma dropped that orange flier off, and I could have sworn that I threw it away. But next day I found it in a different part of the office. It was in the little lobby area toward the front in among the old copies of *Newsweek* and *Highlights*. I picked it up and got all puzzled for a moment or two.

Next day I found it again, this time by the fax machine, and I was standing there looking at it, just as Jonathan Bale, my adolescent-looking attorney, came through the door. He was wearing a frisky, light-colored spring suit, his boyish hair swished this way and that. I had been working with his attorney friend Randy Talley on the courtroom end of things.

Jonathan asked me how I was liking working with Randy, and I said I liked him just fine. We'd had a couple meetings in preparation for the case.

"Is that for the Shakespeare Festival?" he asked, noticing the orange flier in my hands.

"Yeah, it's the weirdest thing, I thought I threw it away," I said.

"Sandy, my wife, was in that a couple years ago," he said. "Let's see . . . seems like it was Midsummer Dream something. Midsummer Night Dream. I don't think I got it right—anyway, it was fun."

"She liked it?"

"Oh—she had a blast," he enthused.

"Is she trying out again?"

"No," he laughed, "She's out to here!" He made a big, ballooning gesture at his stomach.

"She's pregnant? Sandy's pregnant?"

His smile was a mile wide. "Yeah, she sure is."

"Oh, that's great. That's really fantastic."

"She feels like Godzilla," he said. "It's our second."

"Yeah, you're always bigger with your second," I said. "Or so I've heard. My sister, Peggy, I remember she was huge—huuuuuge—with her second."

"Yeah, so anyway," Jonathan said, "she loved the festival. Thought it was real positive."

Chapter 10

"That's what Gemma Nichols says, she's the one who brought this thing by."

"Yeah, Gemma was in Midsummer with Sandy. I think she played the fairy queen or something."

"Really?"

"Yeah. They were all flitting around in little, gauzy green dresses of one kind or another."

I stopped for a moment, thinking over my brief meeting with Gemma. "She seems a little . . ."

"She's a funky gal," Jonathan said. "She's definitely from a different planet."

"Does she strike you that way? I'm such a barbarian, I think everyone's a little funky."

"No, Gemma's one-of-a-kind," Jonathan said, nodding vigorously. "She's a doozy. She was in here talking about the universe—"

"Yep."

"And golden orbs—"

"Yep."

"And energy stored in various places in your body—"

"That's her."

"I guess I'm not around that kind of stuff much."

"But Gemma's a sweetheart. She really is. I know you guys are technically in competition, but she's second to none. Really," and he grinned and laughed, "next to you, of course."

"Right. Sure."

This is how it usually went with Jonathan and me—all in good spirits. Jonathan spoke with me briefly about some dirt he'd dug up on Bernard Hunt. Sure enough, old Hunt was in financial arrears and needed very much to get out of purchasing the Pompidou property.

"I'm afraid it's just business; he probably had every intention of buying the place and then got caught up short," Jonathan said. "You just got caught in the middle of it."

I sat against my desk feeling tired and lifeless. "I'm the monkey's uncle," I groaned.

"I ran this all by Randy today," Jonathan said.

"What'd he say?"

"Well, you need to talk to him. But I think it's time to start thinking about how to protect your assets."

"From bankruptcy," I said.

He nodded. Very serious.

"Oh, boy," I sighed.

"If I were you, I'd move as much of your assets out of the business as possible. Because that's where it's going to hit."

"But what about the punitive damages," I said. "Punitive! That's personal. That's my pocketbook."

"Well...that's where we've got some wiggle room," he said. "That's less likely to hit you than the business. The court is not as likely to let him go after your personal finances as your business. Now understand, this is all speculation. It could all change in court."

"Why did he include the personal punitive stuff, then?"

"To scare you. To get you serious. Maybe to get you to settle out of court. That's really the easiest for both of you. Things like this get real messy and real unpredictable in front of a judge. Most civil actions end up getting settled out of court."

I thought this through for a moment. "Can I countersue?"

"For what?"

"Breach of contract."

His head fell to one side, considering the idea momentarily. Then he shook his head. "I doubt it. Talk to Randy? But I doubt it."

"I should be able to sue him for emotional distress," I said. A heaviness coming over me. "I should be able to sue him for making my life a living hell."

"I know," Jonathan said gently. He took my arm and rubbed it up and down in a sympathetic way.

"This makes my head hurt."

"Talk to Randy and get back in touch with me, OK?"

I nodded. "OK."

When he left, the office was real quiet. I looked out the front windows on a street full of tourists in their little tourist hats, their tourist sunglasses. Smiling, holding hands, window shopping. Everyone on Main Street was swept away in the glory of spring.

I had to get out into that. Had to do something to shake off this gloom and doom. So I grabbed my sack lunch and locked up the office and got in my car. I drove out of town and soon found myself at the turnoff to the Pompidou property. I made the turn and drove slowly up the dirt drive, around the long bend, and took a deep breath when the meadow opened wide in front of me. Past the schoolhouse and the stand of ever-

Chapter 10

greens beyond, there was the ocean, huge and blue.

I parked in front of the schoolhouse and got out and sat on the front steps. The warm sun beamed down on me; the sound of the breeze blew through the grass. Way overhead, a red-tailed hawk caught an updraft, and with its wings spread, rode the air, holding its position, resting on a pillow of wind. What must that be like? I wondered. To be a bird half-sleeping on air.

Suddenly I loved being alive again. I loved the feel of life. It all came back to me, what it was like as a girl waking up on a spring morning, the whole rambunctious day ahead of me.

I slowly unwrapped my sandwich and pulled a can of apple juice out of my lunch bag. This was living. My teeth sank into the thick, wheaty hull of the bread, and there inside was the sweet acidic strawberry jam I'd spread thickly that morning.

I ate quietly, letting my mind go, thinking about that hawk ... and Bernard Hunt and all the civil cases in all the courts in all the world ... and Gemma Nichols ... and the universe.

The universe, my little piece of it, was so complicated; imagine multiplying that by all the people on this planet, and you realize that the angels have a big-sized job on their hands. A giant, restless river of gold between heaven and earth.

When I'd finished eating, I stood up and spanked imaginary dirt off my skirt. I entered the schoolhouse, taking in it its creaky old peacefulness. Then I saw it.

A breath caught in my throat. Not again.

Up on that little stage area, someone had repainted that pentagram in red on the far wall. Bigger this time than the one I'd scraped away back in April, the five-pointed star inside a crudely spray-painted circle. Drips of red paint drizzled down to the floor like blood from a wound that refused to heal. A chill snaked through me. This was some kind of act of defiance. A shatter to my pool of meditation.

Someone had returned and had left this diabolical symbol behind as if to say "You can't stop us."

"We'll just see about this," I said to myself.

I hoisted myself up on the stage, and I grabbed a broken stick and wedged it into the layer of old, damp plaster and began to pry it away from the wood underneath.

Chunks of the old white stuff came off pretty easily, and I found myself chiseling and gouging away with vigor. A sense of motherly

protectiveness rose up in me as I did this—feeling as though someone had defaced my own home.

The pentagram was about four feet wide, four feet tall, and by the
time I'd chipped away a good portion of it—and the bare, ribbed lath
underneath was exposed—I made a startling discovery.

A straight up-and-down seam revealed itself in the woodwork.

I stopped for a moment and followed the seam with my finger. As I
stooped down, I saw that the vertical seam was reflected as a slight crack
in the plaster. It ran all the way to the floor. Then I straightened up and
followed the tiny crack to about six feet off the floor where it made a
90-degree left turn and made a straight-across line about three feet long
and made another sharp turn down toward the floor.

I stood back, taking it all in. In short, the seam formed the outline
of a door. A door on this far wall had been plastered over.

I grabbed my broken stick and followed the seam, prying the plaster away, and after another ten or fifteen minutes' work, I had dug a
little canal following the seam and uncovered the entire thing. Then
I pressed the stick under the center of the pentagram, and with a
levering motion, managed to dislodged a large piece of moist plaster
away in a single, wobbly chunk. The chunk crashed to the floor, and
I waved away the dust.

Sure enough, behind all that clutter, I'd found a door.

My nightmare—I took a step backward—a sudden sense of weak-
ness and faltering nerves. I remembered my dream—the nightmare
where Dan Hanson and I had been running and running down long,
dark tunnels from an unseen beast. And finally we'd run up against
a pentagram. And the pentagram had been a doorway. I'd said to
Dan, "We have to go through this," but he had refused.

I stood there looking at my discovery—this was no dream. Here
was that doorway.

Though I was alone, I felt as though someone was watching me. I
was out there by myself in that old schoolhouse, but someone out
in "the universe" was waiting for my next move.

I became aware of each breath I took, of a thickness in my throat,
of my urge to run . . .

And yet, how could I stop now? Here it was, something from a
dreamworld beckoning to me.

I wedged the stick behind the remainder of the plaster, and in
minutes, I'd gotten it all unstuck from the wall. Now the door was

there, plain as could be. It had no knob or handle; it wasn't even a door, really. Just a doorframe that had been blocked off with newer lath work.

I pushed against it, and the thing gave a little.

I went out to my car and rummaged around in the trunk. The blaze of sunshine outside gave me a little kick of courage.

In the trunk I found a tire iron, and I took it back inside.

One of the four prongs on the cross-shaped tire iron was a wedge for prying off hubcaps, and I jammed it into the seam in the wood. I gave a solid push and felt a solid, cement resistance. I pushed again. Nothing.

So I changed tactics by wiggling the wedge in deeper and pulling the iron toward me, in essence pressing the door inward. This time the thing gave a little. What a wonderful feeling that is—that first hint of victory. I pulled again. And again. And again. Finally I heard the splintering of wood, the squawk of studs against nailheads. I worked and worked at it, sweat coming to my face and back.

Finally I'd worked the blocked-off part away from the main wall and gave it a shove with my shoulder. It yielded to my pressure. One-half of the thing opened wide enough so that I was able shove some more and create a good-sized entryway. Keeping the tire iron in my hand, I stuck my head inside. It was a small, dark, airless, mildew-smelling room. And I could see the problem; it wasn't just that the doorway was hammered shut; I was pushing against what looked like a heap of garbage.

In the dim light, I could make out vague shapes of stacks of news-paper and jumbles of fabric and box shapes. Odd and ends. Still I pushed and gradually made a little progress against the trash. Then working this way and that, I got my whole body through the open-ing and found myself in that secret space.

Finding blocked off rooms or spaces in old buildings like the schoolhouse is not out-of-this-world unusual. Most often you find that old fireplaces have been blocked off. Sometimes very large ones. As a real estate agent, I've seen old rooms blocked off for lots of rea-sons. In one decrepit farmhouse, a former occupant had sealed off an entire parlor, simply because the flooring was so rotten it was cheaper to block the doorway than to fix the floor.

But even knowing all that could not diminish the fact that my chest felt small, my breaths were short. Blood pumped hard in my neck. This was Indiana Jones exciting.

Who knows when anyone had last been inside this room. My mind raced through what little I knew of the schoolhouse.

It'd been built in the middle of the 1800s and had probably served as both a school and a church for a small mining community. Later when the ramshackle town disbanded, someone had lived here. Seems like an old woman had died here in the 1960s and—if what Brenda Ann and the trustee had told me was correct—a low-budget horror movie of some kind had been filmed out here.

That was the extent of my knowledge—and any of that could be untrue.

The room was not large, probably no more than about six feet deep by fifteen or twenty feet wide—about the same width as the stage. I felt around in the darkness and—

—hot, slicing sting.

I cried out and yanked my hand back.

There could be scorpions back here. You idiot, I lectured myself, didn't even bother to think about that!

Scorpions and black widows and all kinds of poisonous things.

I held my hand in the light of the doorway. On my ring finger there was a razor thin cut. Warm, runny blood was all over my fingers and trickling quickly down into my palm.

Wow, that hurt. It wasn't a deep cut, but you have a lot of blood vessels in your fingers.

I clenched my fist to hold in the blood, I didn't want to wipe it on my skirt. That cut really stung, and I knew I should go take care of it, but my eyes were starting to adjust to the darkness. The heaps of trash were at about waist deep. I could see where the cut had come from—a box that had been torn open was full of old, broken canning jars. Cruel, jagged, glass tips pointed upward.

To my right I found what looked like a stack of old newspapers. I hesitated picking them up because I imagined rats and silverfish in abundance back there. I needed a flashlight. But working up my courage, I picked one up with my good hand. The damp paper peeled away. Part of the soggy paper underneath came with it, tearing silently. I turned back to the doorway where the light came in.

I found that I held a sodden newspaper from 1959. A section of the San Francisco Chronicle. The front page heralded various stories of the day, nothing of outstanding interest. But it gave me an idea of how long the room had been sealed off.

Chapter 10

As I shuffled around, I became aware of the fact that the floor did not feel very stable. Under my feet, it bowed in a springy sort of way, and a wave of panicky goosebumps swept all over me. I turned around the other direction—*augh!*

A large, corded spiderweb caught my face, and I hooted and yelled and batted it away with the wet newspaper.

I squeezed back through the newly opened doorway and into the relative light and roominess of the small stage. The pentagram lay in plaster chunks at my feet.

I had to leave. I had to get out. I still held that newspaper, and with same hand I grabbed the tire iron.

A sharp, insistent sense of peril pushed me off the stage and hustled me out into the welcoming rays of the sun.

Whew. I stood there breathing air that smelled of spring grass instead of mildew. Out under a bright blue sky.

I looked at the newspaper in my hands. July 2, 1959. Wow! is all I could think. This was crazy.

I went to the trunk of my car again, where I put away the tire iron, and I found a small towel and wrapped my bloody hand in it.

I walked around outside for a while, feeling the need to get my bearings. I liked this wide-open meadow very much, and I liked the schoolhouse. It was all infused with a sense of pioneering and of new worlds to be conquered.

I calmed down and got in the car and started up and just sat there for a moment. The sense of danger had passed, and I gripped the steering wheel, enjoying a whole new feeling.

Elation.

Complete, unfiltered, unpasteurized, raw elation. I'd been so scared at first. That doorway, seeming to emerge from the pentagram. A thing foretold in a dark dreamworld.

It must be how mountain climbers feel when they've successfully reached the summit. To place yourself in harm's way—and to have beaten it. The boldness I felt. The triumph!

I knew I had to come back. I had to come back with a flashlight, and I had to go back through that doorway. Maybe I'd find nothing more than newspapers and broken canning jars . . . it hardly mattered.

I looked back at that old school building, felt a smile-sensation all through me—we were a team, we old gals. We were meant to be.

CHAPTER
11

As I said before, once an idea takes up residence in your brain, funny things start to happen. My perspective on life took a turn—I mean to tell you, the blinker went on, and the wheels turned, and zoom, off I went—and there I was on the Yellow Brick Road zipping off into a new horizon. At quite a clip.

The sense of doom vanished. That old, tired, defeated feeling was no more.

I found myself waking in the morning with high-flying energy, the gears in my brain turning and whizzing. I attacked everything. I attacked my breakfast. I attacked the dishes. I attacked my car when it was time to go to town.

I became obsessed with feeling all of life around me, down to the smallest detail. I fell in love with the way thick socks felt on cold evenings, and I rejoiced at the sting of mint toothpaste and listened for the muffled rat-tat-tat sound of tearing off a good, stout paper towel. Bird songs and blinking, the crunch of ice in my molars and haylike scent of cantaloupe rind in the market. All these became causes for rejoicing.

I became convinced that all the little threads of my life were coming together toward a happy meeting point.

And it all came together at that schoolhouse. At least, according to the two attorneys in my life.

I remember trying to explain it all to Peggy—what Jonathan was

Chapter 11

calling "The Grand Plan." One afternoon later in June, I went out to check on her. Walking into "the great room," there she was, still doing her mad-widow act. Looking all spinstery with an orange afghan over her knees, sipping tea out of a dirty mug, watching nothing particular on television. Sunlight made the lace-covered windows glow in rectangular sheets of white gold.

"You're looking like an outpatient," I said.

She gave me a look of longsuffering and coughed into her tiny fist for effect.

"I'm all right," she complained.

"You've still got that cough," I said loudly. I realized I was speaking to her like you speak to a deafened elderly person.

"You're being that way again," she said.

"What way?"

"Acting like I'm 102."

You didn't get much past Peggy.

"Well," I said. "It's just that you're sitting here with that silly afghan over yourself in the middle of June. You look like Grandma Moses."

She was quiet, even pensive for a moment. "It used to bother me that you didn't visit more often ... but now ..." she chided.

"Oh, come on," I said.

She remarked on how fired-up I seemed. And I said I was doing better.

I told her how both the attorneys, Jonathan Bale and Randy Talley, had cooked up a plan to help yours truly not only to avoid debtors prison but also to build toward a sound financial future. It pays to have a good attorney.

Since the lawsuit hadn't even come before a judge yet, there were ways—if I acted immediately—to finagle things in my favor.

There's always wiggle room, they told me.

The problem was, it was a deal with the devil, because it involved my surrendering a couple of things that were very precious to me.

One was my condo.

The other was my business.

The two attorneys explained the lawsuit, if won, could end up putting a lien on my business and condo.

On the other hand, if we settled out of court, it would mean the trustee would have to give back the money from the sale, and I would have to give back my commission. In all likelihood, this would wind up meaning that the trustee could take me to court.

It was a two-fisted thing.

So Randy and Jonathan sat back and gazed at the ceiling and plucked their suspenders for an afternoon and came up with a complex deal involving reams of paper and legal blah, blah, blah. But in the end, the plan we created meant selling the business and the condo and taking that money and satisfying an out-of-court settlement directly to Bernard Hunt so that the trustee wouldn't have to fork over her money. And then in a mind-boggling complicated scheme, the property would be deeded over to me.

"It's simply a transfer of assets," Jonathan had explained. "You convert your business and condo to cash and transfer that to Bernard Hunt. Then he in turn agrees to relinquish claim to the deed on the property, and the trustee, in turn, re-deeds the property to you."

"It's a shell game," I protested.

"Yes," he said patiently. "It's a shell game. But it'll keep you from losing your shirt."

So I would own the Pompidou property myself. I had fallen in love with that place, anyway. Why not? Then I could invest my savings to renovating the schoolhouse as best I could.

A person could turn that schoolhouse into a dreamhouse with a little spit and polish. A little sweat equity. It's just the project I needed.

With that ocean view, getting that building out of its condemned state—let a few years go by, let the market rise a little more, I could eventually walk away with a handsome sack of cash.

After working out the deal on paper, Jonathan and I had spoken with the trustee, and she was mulling over the plan. So I might get out of the real estate market as a broker, but I could still be in it as an owner. As an investor.

"Sounds iffy," Peggy said, when I attempted to explain the deal. "What if this Bernard Punt doesn't want to settle out of court."

"Bernard Hunt," I corrected.

She gave me a dismissive wave. "You know what I mean."

"Well, if he wants to take this thing to court, then it all falls apart, and I'm living on the street."

"You could always move in with us," she said.

"No, I couldn't," I corrected her.

"You won't have a choice."

"I'd panhandle on Main Street before I'd move in here," I said.

Chapter 11

"You would not. You're too vain."

"Too vain to move in under your roof," I huffed.

"Oh, get over yourself," she muttered.

"Besides," I said, "my lawyer says that the only reason this guy lodged the suit against me anyway is because he doesn't have the money to buy the place. Jonathan did a little sleuthing around and found out that this guy lost a bunch of money in the stock market, and he's a big gambler to boot. Throws his money around."

"Which means what?" Peggy asked.

"Which means that he just wants to get out of the deal. And if he can get out of the deal and get his money back, he'll do it. He doesn't have the time or the resources to really drag this thing through the courts."

"Then why not call his bluff?" she asked. "Let him take you to court."

"Because I don't have the time or resources either."

"And you think all this scheming and planning will pay off?"

"It's my best shot," I said. "You have a better plan?"

Peggy's mouth twitched this way and that. She was methodically thinking her way through this dilemma. "What'll you do for work in the meantime?" she wanted to know.

"In the meantime, I'll pick something up. Maybe I could drive one of these tourist buses, or I could get an office job at the college, or . . . shoot . . . I could lay low for a while and then go work for another Realtor."

Peggy frowned and glared into her tea mug. "So you're just gonna go from one thing to the other, then," she croaked, disapprovingly.

"What's . . ." I started. Then cocked my head. "What do you mean?"

She gave a frail shrug. "It's what you do."

"What—you—are you trying to be insulting? What're you yapping about, 'it's what I do.' What's that mean?"

"You always just go from one thing to another. A flibbertijibbet. It's the way you've always been. Always."

"A what? What'd you I say I was?" I said, getting steamed up.

Another meek shrug from Peggy that meant "Don't shoot the messenger."

"What's . . . what's a flibbertiwhatzit?"

"A flibbertijibbet. It's just a . . . I don't know. Look it up."

My eyes felt like they were gonna blow right outta my head. "I

99

will," I said. "That's exactly what I'm gonna do, you old crone."

"Crone," she muttered.

I searched through the bookshelves until I found my father's giant old dictionary. I hefted it over to a table and flipped through the old yellowed pages.

I found flibbertijibbet, and my mouth dropped. I was flabbergasted. I announced the definition, "A gossiping, frivolous, chattering, restless person."

She nodded her head and kept watching the TV.

"You're saying that I'm a frivolous, chattering . . . gossiping person?"

"I'm only telling you the truth. You can never stick to one thing."

I sat in a chair. Just fell into the thing like a sack of bricks. "How can you say that? You shock me. You really do."

"A shock?" she said. "Maybe to you."

"I can't believe this. You—it wasn't but two months ago you were telling me about this New Roses thing. This idea that one thing is taken away from you and another comes in its place."

"That's not quite it."

"That's exactly it!"

"I said God takes away one thing, and then He brings something else in its place."

"All right, fine, split hairs."

"You left God out of it."

"No, I didn't."

She twisted around to face me. "You did, Merideth. You left God out of it. God gives us New Roses . . . things don't just happen. Nothing just happens. We're led to things. Doors open. You're so flip about things that are so important."

"I'm not flip."

"You are. You are flip. Your husband died, and you buried your belief in God with him. You turned your back on Him. And I can't sit here and stay silent about it. Look at what your life's been since Simon died. It's all been about your anger at God."

"Give me a break."

"You said it to me when he died. You said to me, 'How could God let me fall in love with a man who was going to die?' Those are your words."

"I said that in a moment of pain. A moment of deep, deep pain."

"A moment of honesty," she grumbled.

"Of course, you have to throw it back in my face."

Again, I got the shrug. "I have to say these things. I'm not well. I have to say the things that need to be said. I can't pussyfoot around anymore."

She turned and gazed at the TV.

"Peggy . . ."

"What?"

"What do you mean you're not well? Are you just being dramatic?"

"I don't know. I don't think so. I don't feel good, Mer. I always feel poorly, and I can't ever seem to knock this cough."

"But you're taking your medication, right?"

"Yes."

"And it's not helping?"

Her head bobbed side to side. "It seemed to help right at first. But it feels different than anything I've had before. Remember when I had that walking pneumonia?"

"Yeah."

"This feels different. It feels like it's attached to my bones. I can't explain it."

"What does your doctor say?"

"I see her again on Thursday . . ."

A loud commercial was blaring from the television. I stood up, "Can I turn this thing off?" I said, bending toward the off button.

"No! Don't!" she cried. "Marc's on in a second."

"Marc?"

"Yes, he called and said he got a part on this soap opera."

"Oh, boy," I groaned.

For years, her son, Marc, had been down in L.A. trying to make it big in TV and movies. Once he was in a truck commercial, just for a split second, and then about a year previous, he'd been on a show about animals. He introduced segments about monkeys and flamingos on a special about zoo animals.

I watched this soap opera for a few minutes. Serious-faced blonde actresses flitting around with serious-faced steely-jaws actors.

"Here we go," Peggy said.

The scene was in a dark, harbor-side restaurant. A young woman with sucked-in cheeks was flirting with a dark-haired, thin-faced Satan-looking guy at the bar. There was some kind of forbidden passion on the horizon. She was married, or he was married, or something along that line.

Then we saw Marc in the background. He was the bartender. He wore a crisp white shirt and a tidy black vest. He was vigorously drying drink glasses with a towel.

"He looks a little older on TV," I said to Peggy.

She nodded. "I can't believe he's playing a bartender, he doesn't even drink," she said, her face souring. "He's against drinking, and there he is playing a bartender."

She sighed.

On the television, things were warming up between the man and the woman.

Man: I like a challenge (lifting his glass without drinking, giving a cockeyed smirk, eyebrows wiggling suggestively).

Woman: Do you? (giving her own cockeyed smirk).

Man: Oh yes. (He drank and ice tinkled in his glass.)

Woman: Does it seem hot in here all of a sudden?

Man: I don't know. (He turns to the barkeep, Marc.) Hey, does it seem hot in here to you?

Marc: (looks up, lips pouted a little) Indeed it does.

Woman: (glances at Marc) Maybe you could open a window?

Marc: (frowns in a friendly way) As the lady wishes.

Man: (turns back to the woman, his voice all smoky) You've got a lot of pull around here.

Woman: (her voice all smoky) Let's go out on the terrace and see the stars.

Man: As the lady wishes.

I looked over at Peggy, who was shaking her head.

I turned away and groaned. "Oh . . . that's just sad. Is that what Marc does for a living?"

Peggy nodded. "He says he does this stuff to pay his bills. He's involved in a Christian theater group in L.A. I have their brochure around here," she said, looking around the room, as if it might be tacked up on the wall. She didn't locate it. "Well, anyway, they're called Crossways. Something like that. But I wish he wouldn't do this kind of thing. It's tacky."

I shrugged. "Well, I'm gonna go. I'm gonna go off and flit from one thing to another."

"Merideth," she said, full of rebuke.

"I'm not like you," I said. "When Simon died, I grieved. I was in a state, but I moved on. I moved on to other things. I can't just waste

Chapter 11

away," I said, indicating her little withered body sitting in that chair. "I can't play the grieving widow forever. Life goes on for me."

"You've forsaken God."

"I haven't. And I resent you saying that."

"When was the last time you went to church?"

"When was the last time you went?" I snapped.

"I watch it on TV."

"You watch church on TV," I retorted sarcastically. "Why? Are you a cripple? Did someone sew your rear end to that chair?"

She was silent for a moment. And I felt bad for trouncing her like that. She was delicate in her way, and I was angry with God in my way. I just didn't want her to be right. She was always the older sister, even now. Always the voice of conscience. And in her mad-widow way, she did, even now, have an aura of wisdom about her.

"I pray for you," she said. "Turn that thing off," indicating the TV.

I moved forward and snapped it off, and the room got very quiet.

"I pray for you each and every day," she continued. "I want you to know that God will not let you go. No matter how you scorn Him, no matter how you curse Him, your name is always before Him. In the throne room of heaven, angels weep when they hear your name."

I wasn't sure what to say.

"I pray for you too," I said. "I do. I pray for you and Brenda Ann and little Brady and even Marc."

She had a faraway look, gazing into the glow of the lace in the window. "Marc," she said.

CHAPTER
12

The day finally came when I locked up my real estate office for the last time. And it didn't matter that I'd worked out a smart financial plan with Randy Talley and Jonathan Bale, and it didn't matter that we'd settled with Bernard Hunt out of court. It didn't matter that the East Coast trustee had agreed to deed me the Pompidou property.

Jonathan had gone above and beyond the call of duty—he'd given me a temporary job. Normally, his wife would run his law office, file things, get documents from the courts and whatnot. Since she was pregnant, she wanted to take it easy, and he needed help. So I became his office manager. It was very flexible. A few hours a day. A few days a week. Whatever, it didn't matter when I came or went. And he paid generously.

Still, money wasn't at the heart of my sadness.

I had loved being a real estate agent. I had loved being my own boss. I had loved pulling myself up by my own bootstraps.

When I pushed the key into the lock and gave it a turn and heard that bolt snap shut, something inside me was forever changed.

It was like turning that last page in a book you really, really love. You don't want it to be over. And like that favorite book, you know you can never read it again for the first time.

I could never start up my own business again for the first time. I could never again go from the darkness of Simon's death into the light of day without saying, "Yes, I've done this before."

I pulled the key out, and I stood away from the glass door, still looking inside. Seeing the empty space that used to be Merideth Dill Real Estate. The desk, the furniture and magazines in the lobby area, and the little pictures that had hung on the walls were gone. It was now just an empty commercial space. It was going to be leased out to become a women's shoe boutique.

My eyes refocused for a moment, and there was my face reflected in the glass door. The face of a disappointed forty-eight-year-old woman. A woman who should be a mother. Should be a wife. Should live in a neat, three-bedroom home filled with mementos and pictures of graduations and summer camps.

I couldn't even hang onto a man. There I was, a woman who'd killed off her first husband. And scared off the next decent man by refurnishing his house when he wasn't looking.

Couldn't hang on to a business.

A flibbertigibbet.

Since that conversation with Peggy, I'd learned where she'd heard that word. It's in a song from that movie *The Sound of Music.* Little Julie Andrews plays a flighty nun, and the other nuns in the abbey sing of her, "a flibbertigibbet, a will o' the wisp, a clown . . ."

A clown.

That fit the description of the face reflected in that glass doorway.

A clown. And I didn't even have to wear a big red nose to prove it.

I pulled the key out of the lock and got in my car and drove away into an unknown future.

CHAPTER
13

I had sold my condo in order to satisfy the terms of "The Grand
Plan" to stave off Bernard Hunt and poverty and shame.

Of course, that left me in a pickle. Because I now had no permanent residence.

"You should move in with us," Brenda Ann said to me.

She'd come over one morning to the condo to help me pack, but
we mostly ended up sitting around and eating. I found two boxes of
brownie mix and a box of pancake mix, and it seemed stupid to haul
them around with me. So we were sitting in among piles of boxes
eating brownies and pancakes. Oh, and dried prunes. I'd found a car-
ton of dried prunes.

"I can't live with you," I said. "There's already you and Brady and
your mom in that house. And when Marc comes up—you think I
wanna be around that?"

"But it's just temporary," she said. "Don't be dumb. Come on."

"I'm not being dumb at all," I countered. "Ninety percent of a
happy family involves not living together. You know that."

"But we'd like to have you there. You should have just moved in
to begin with—why did you buy that place out there?" she said, almost in alarm. "You know what a creepy place that is. You're just
inviting trouble."

"No, I'm not."

"You are. You totally know what kind of stuff went on out there.

You totally know! All that chicken blood, Satan stuff. You're just lucky I haven't told Mom about it."

"And you shouldn't," I cautioned. "She wouldn't understand."

"Of course she wouldn't understand, because she's not stupid!"

I took a bite of a brownie and leaned back. I looked at this young kid with the ring in her nose, with her tank top, her army boots, her unwashed hippie hair, and I said to her, "You know, you and your mother are more alike than I ever realized."

"That's not—" she laughed, catching crumbs falling out of her mouth. "That's not even close to being true."

"Why?"

She smirked. "Look at me. I'm not exactly the picture of my mother."

"Yeah, I know. You're right on the money. That's exactly it. You look different than your mom. You go out and buy all these scraggly, scrap-heap clothes, and you don't wash your hair or style it, and you poke that stupid ring in your nose, but you know? I think that's all just to throw people off."

She laughed and shook her head. Her mouth was too full of brownies and prunes to answer.

"It's true," I pressed on. "And one of these days, the deception will end."

"The deception!" she cried.

"Yes, you'll stop being afraid of all that. You'll stop being scared of being like her, and when that happens, we're gonna see a big change—a BIG change in you."

"That is not true," she said.

"No see, what you don't understand yet at nineteen is that the way people dress or fix their hair—that's not all there is. That can change. It's the attitudes inside that give it all away. On the outside, you are a hippy-dippy woman of the nineties. On the inside, you're as much your mother as anyone I've ever met."

She smiled, but it was a stiff-lipped expression of annoyance. Her old aunt had crossed a line. Brenda Ann looked away and sucked in her upper lip and bit her thumb and then looked back over at me.

"That's just not true," she said.

"Time will tell," I said.

"I do wash my hair," she said. "Hey, what's happening with you and Dan Hanson?" she asked. Changing the subject.

I smiled. "You're changing the subject."

"I know," she said.

"Well, let's see, what's happening with me and Professor Hanson? Not much, to tell the truth."

"I thought you called him."

"I did. I said we should get together for lunch today."

"Really?" Her face was full of delight and surprise. "Today?"

"Sure, why not?"

"Gonna rekindle the flame?"

I wiped my face with a napkin. "Nothing to rekindle. We were never more than friends. You know that."

"I don't know that," she said. "You really liked him. You were his decorator."

"Well, it takes two to tango," I said.

"But you're still seeing him," she pointed out.

"Not really. We haven't gotten together in a coon's age."

Her face changed. "Oops, there's my beeper," she said, reaching around to her pocket.

"You're ruled by that thing," I said.

"I know," without apology. She looked intently at the read-out screen. "I gotta go."

I glanced around at all the boxes and heaps around the room. "Can you help me later on?" I asked. "This is a doozy of a job ahead of me."

"Yeah, of course."

When Brenda left, I hopped in the car and drove over to my newly rented studio apartment at "Green Ash Gardens." I had taken this pocket-sized apartment while work was going on out at the school-house. By now I'd taken a tour out there with a general contractor who specialized in "resurrection," as he put it. His name was Fowler Hayden.

"Fowler Hayden," I had smirked at our first meeting, looking at his business card. "Is that your real name?"

He gave a big gap-toothed grin and adjusted the bill of his badly weathered hat. "Yeah, 'at's what my mama gave me. It's a family name from way back."

Fowler Hayden was a short drink of water with a bulldog face, and on those brief occasions where he removed his cap, he was bald as a whale. He'd only lived in Green Ash a few years, but everyone told me he was a sharp operator. In a town where your reputation counted for everything, he was a contractor without blemish. That's rare.

And he wasn't too pricey. So I felt like I was doing OK.

My temporary housing was a studio that basically amounted to a side room in a giant Victorian near downtown, an old historic mansion that had been cordoned off into four or five apartments. Large redwood trees provided dark, scented shade out front and along the sides of the house. Out front I ran into the landlord, a young woman named Katy. Her cute little two-year-old, Howie, was in a stroller gnawing on a rubber toy. We agreed that I would rent the place month-to-month until I could vacate and take up residence in the schoolhouse.

After running more errands, it was lunch time, and I went to the Mexican place, Tres Hombres, where Dan and I went so often. A petite red-haired waitress named Liz recognized me and said Hi. I got there before Dan did, and Liz showed me to a table.

"I'm waiting for a friend," I said.

"Uh-huh, that tall guy?"

"Yes."

"He better not stand you up," she said. "I'll give him the what for."

"Me, too," I said.

I ordered a soda and waited. And waited.

The place gradually filled up for lunch. I saw a few people I'd known from way back. Several stopped by and said Hi, asked what I was up to these days, and I brought a smile to my face and talked about renovating the schoolhouse on the Pompidou property and talked about working with the people at the historical commission to make sure I was in compliance with them.

They all expressed relief that that old property had ended up in the hands of a local like myself and not an out-of-towner who'd just turn it into a weekend party house.

After I finished my soda and was looking hungrily over the menu for the twentieth time, Liz came up and said I had a phone call.

"It's a man," she sang, rolling her eyes.

I followed her to the kitchen entrance where she hit the hold button and handed the phone to me.

"Merideth, it's Dan."

"Yes?" I said.

"Look . . ." discomfort in his voice, "I forgot I have a faculty meeting to go to. I'm sorry. Really. I can't get out of it."

"That's OK, Dan."

"I could get out of it, but I shouldn't. I need to be there. It's an end-of-school-year thing."

I know how that goes," I said.

"We'll get together again soon."

He apologized quietly and sincerely and that was that. I wasn't hungry, really, but I went back to my table. Some part of my imagination construed all kinds of devious male reasons why he wasn't coming. But finally, I just figured I had to let it rest. Even if Dan was making something up, it was best that he not come if he felt uncomfortable.

How I hate being so logical. So fair.

Still, I could be an adult. I could eat lunch alone. It was no big deal, I told myself woefully.

"Hi, there," a cheerful voice said.

I looked up. It was Gemma Nichols. She looked tanned and jubilant and pixieish, looking like she'd hopped down from a little cloud somewhere.

"Are you eating alone?" she asked.

"Well—"

"I hate eating alone. Could I join you? Would you mind too much?"

"Not at all," I half-lied.

She smiled gratefully and sat down, and we shot the breeze about this, that, and the other. But my heart really wasn't in it. When you're in the real estate business, you become a professional chatterbox. But I wasn't in the business anymore... kinda took the spunk out of me...

We both ordered some lunch, and the food quickly arrived.

"You seem a little ... downish," Gemma said.

"Yeah?"

"Yes, you do."

I took this to mean that she now hoped I would start spilling my guts. It was girl talk time. But I wasn't sure I was up for that. Gemma was still a stranger to me. And in some ways a little bit of a threat to my bruised self because of her easy success. At least it seemed easy from where I was sitting.

"I ... I don't like to ..." I waved my hand in the air as if brushing away my troubles like so many twittering gnats, "I'm not one to go on and on about ... you know ... things."

"You don't like to talk about your issues," she said with a slow blink of disappointment.

"Gotta keep the mystery," I said.

Gemma laughed a little. "Mysterious womanhood," she said in an amused murmur.

I nodded with all the wisdom of the ages. "Mysterious womanhood," I agreed.

"Well. That's just OK with me. Because I'll just bet I can figure out what's wrong," she said. Her purse was hanging on the back of her seat, and she retrieved it. She reached inside and pulled out a small packet of something wrapped in a purple silk scarf.

As I watched, she laid the small bundle on the table and carefully unwrapped it. When the scarf was open, in the center lay a pile of curious-looking cards. The card on top had an odd, brightly colored design, a goat, stars, and angels. I couldn't quite make it out.

"Do you ever do tarot?" Gemma asked.

"Tarot cards?" I asked. A funny leap happened in my guts. And I felt myself shift away from her. "Um . . . no."

She sensed my discomfort. "Are you OK with this? I just want to do a quick reading on you. Is that all right?"

"What do you do with those things?"

"Here," she handed me the deck. "Just shuffle them and concentrate on whatever it is that's bothering you. Go ahead."

I hesitated. I glanced around the restaurant. No one seemed to be paying any attention to us. Why did I feel so nervous? They're just cards, I lectured myself. Nothing more, nothing less.

Pieces of paper.

There was still that flutter in my stomach.

I took the cards and slowly started shuffling them. They were heavier than I'd expected, and they were a little large for my hands, so shuffling them became awkward business. They kept sliding away from me, and I had to pick them up several times.

"I'm not very good at this," I said.

"Doesn't matter. You're doing fine."

"What am I supposed to be doing with them?"

"Just concentrate on your life right now, just focus on things inside of you, the forces around you."

Images began to emerge in my mind's eye . . . Dan Hanson having lunch with me here on that rainy day . . . finding the secret doorway in the schoolhouse ... sweaty Bernard Hunt standing outside of his fancy truck with his girlfriend ... Peggy glaring at me from her chair ... Marc as the soap-opera bartender ... Lots of pictures of people and places flooded through me. Light and dark. Babies in strollers, my father lying in a satin-lined casket ...

"OK, just stop shuffling when you feel finished," Gemma said.

"All right," I was getting the hang of this shuffling stuff. Then I knew somehow that I'd come to the stopping point. I looked up at her. "What now?"

"Hand me the cards."

I gave them back, and she straightened them and then separated them into two, neat piles. Then she grasped the cards that had been on the bottom, and she placed them on top.

"Now pick three."

"Which three?" I asked.

"Doesn't matter. You'll know. They'll come to you."

"What do you mean?"

"Nothing scary. I just mean, you'll pick the right ones."

"How about just the three on top?"

"That's fine. Just slide them off and lay them face up in a row."

I did as she asked and laid them in a row in front of her. She spent a moment studying them.

"This first card is the five of cups," she said.

"Can I see it?"

She handed me the card. It was a painting where five crystal goblets floated above what looked like a pond or something. The whole thing looked like modern art. The background was a rusty orange sunset, but it looked like it was in outer space. The pond was really a pond of stars, and in the corners of the card were angels.

"What's it all supposed to mean?" I asked.

"Well, to start with, because this is the first card in the layout, it means this is a general picture of your past. The five of cups is a minor arcana, and it usually has to do predominantly with disappointment. You can see, if you look carefully, that the cups are in the shape of a pentagram."

I swallowed in a dry throat. "Yes ..."

"Can you see the pentagram shape here?"

Her fingernail tapped the back of the card.

I nodded quickly. A little terrified.

"And as you can see there," she continued, "the cups are empty. At the same time they appear to be ascending upward. Do you see that?"

"Yes."

"So what you've got is a twofold thing. On the one hand there is emptiness, but that emptiness can lead to a greater good—it can symbolize the triumph of the spiritual over the earthly."

"The what over the what?"

"The spiritual over the earthly. Sometimes we come to a place in our lives when we are the most empty, when everything has been taken away from us . . . you know what I mean." She looked at me with a great deal of earnest sympathy.

I nodded and felt a kind of sad nostalgia take hold of me.

She went on: "It's when we're fully empty. That's when we're most able to leave the things of earth behind. Through our emptiness, we ascend. On the one hand, it sounds bad to have everything you love taken from you; on the other hand, it can liberate you." She took a drink of water. "It's like a hot-air balloon. To keep a balloon on the ground, you load it down with ballast. Heavy things. But when you're ready to fly, you have to throw all of that away, you see?"

I nodded.

"Does that make sense?"

"Yes, it makes too much sense," I said quietly, thinking of all those dreams of youth, all those giddy plans of early marriage, all of those bright, happy moments that had slipped away.

"So that's what's behind you. Now the middle card. The middle card can mean where you are right now, or it can mean something you've just recently gone through." She kept her eyes on the card a long time, like she was watching it, seeing if it might move.

"What is it?" I asked.

"This is a powerful one. This is part of the major arcana." She handed the card to me.

Before I could look down, she stared into my eyes. "It's the devil," she said.

"What?" My voice was shrill. I slapped the card down. Face down on the table. "Gemma . . ." Annoyed and disturbed.

"It's not the literal devil, not like what you think."

"It's the devil—for crying out loud," I said.

"Look," she said in a considerate, calming voice, "It's not an evil thing. None of this is about evil. I wouldn't do that to you. The image of the devil is that of a goat. A winged goat from the waist up, a man from the waist down. The card represents a kind of robust, male, dominating force in your recent past."

I nervously licked food remnants off my fingertips. "Like Bernard Hunt," I said.

"Well, there you go. See, the images on the cards? This is all about symbols for things in our lives," she said. "When you dream at night, you don't dream of words, do you."

"Not usually."

"No. We don't dream of reading books; we dream in pictures. That's how our minds work. We think in pictures; we dream in pictures. Look at all the old languages. Egyptians wrote their language as pictures. The Chinese language is all pictures." She smiled and toyed with the drinking straw in her glass. "Do you know what the Chinese character is for strife?"

Her grin was infectious, and I found myself relaxing. "What."

"The Chinese character for strife is a picture of a house with two women in it."

I laughed. "That's why I'm not moving in with my sister. And my niece. I wonder what three women in a house means?"

"I don't know."

"Maybe an explosion or an atomic bomb, something like that," I said.

She nodded. "So anyway, Merideth, if you don't want to do this, that's OK," Gemma said and reached to put the cards away. "You shouldn't do it if you fear it."

"No," I said. "I . . . I'm just not used to this kind of stuff. I always thought it was kinda—out there. You know? Crazy, séancey stuff."

"I know. That's what we're taught to think, but have you ever tried it?"

"No."

"Well if you feel comfortable, why don't you try it, and then make up your mind for yourself?"

"Well . . . that's my usual mode of operation," I said, barking away with more nervous laughter.

"OK, then the middle card, we won't call it by that name that scares you. How's that?" she smirked. "The one you have now represents things like unreasonability, dominance, violence, mood swings, masculine power, chaos, destructiveness."

"All the things we love about men."

"Right," she smiled. "The card tells me there's been a force that's swept through your life like Ghengis Khan and his horde. Does that sound about right?"

"Pretty close."

"But you're going to be all right. You know how I know that?"

"How?"

"First, I look back at our five of cups, your life has been emptied out before," she said. "You've had the stuffin' kicked out of you before, haven't you," she said softly. Gemma reached out and touched my hand. There were tears welling up in her eyes.

I felt a sting in my own eyes and a pang of sorrow move slowly all the way through me. "Yep," I said. "I sure have."

"You're gonna be all right too, because I can see your third card."

"Yeah?" I felt something trickle down my face. It surprised me. It was a tear. An actual tear. The big kind you get when you're eight and you fall off your bike.

"Wow," I said, and used my napkin to dry my face. "I don't know where that came from ..."

Gemma gave my arm a friendly grip. "OK, so on to the future. The third card here is your future, given the direction you're moving in now. Today. The future is always up for change, but given your direction right now ..."

"OK."

"This third one doesn't look so good on the surface, but it's a biggie. It's called the hanged man."

I took the card from her. The main image was an upside down angel. His feet were tied, his arms were outstretched, and his hands had nails in them. His wings looked tattered and droopy. He was the picture of suffering.

"This almost looks like Jesus on the cross," I said. "I mean, he's upside down and he's got wings, but still ..."

"Well, sure, there are similarities to Christian myths," she said. "This hanged man symbolizes redemption through suffering. Now look behind him; you'll see other angels, angels in triumph, and you'll see heavenly light."

"Uh-huh."

"This means that there is a time of difficulty, but when that time is over, there is new life, new understanding, a higher level is attained."

I looked at this card and then at the first one, the five of cups, and I even flipped up one corner of the devil card to confirm something.

"All these cards have angels on them," I said. Surprised.

"It's an angel deck," she said.

"What do you mean an angel deck?"

"Well, there're lots of different tarot decks. I mean, everything. I've seen Egyptian decks, women's healing decks…cat decks…alien decks…American Indian decks…there's the Thoth deck, but you want to stay away from that one."

"How come? What's that?"

"The Thoth deck was created by Alistair Crowley, very dark, a very dark potent force. I won't touch that one."

"Who was Alistair Crowley? Some voodoo guy?"

"He was a highly intelligent but very dark warlock in England. Before he died in the 1930s, newspapers called him the most evil man in the world. He was just so deep into black magic, said to be a very powerful, very dangerous practitioner. Anyway, the upshot is, I don't want to have anything to do with his deck." She reached across the table and picked up my three cards and placed them back with the others. She began rewrapping them with the purple scarf, still talking, "I stick with nice bright things, uplifting things like my angel deck."

I was feeling shaken by all this. Shaken and yet elated. Worked up.

"That was something else," I said.

"So what do you think?" she asked. "Did I do OK?"

"Yeah, I think you did. I think you hit the nail on the head—past, present, and future. Kinda like in that Christmas story with Ebenezer Scrooge. You know how those ghosts show him all those parts of his life."

"*Umm-hmm,*" she nodded then smiled. "I hope it wasn't scary."

"Well, it was," I said. "I feel all willy-nilly."

"You've awakened your energies," she said.

I had no idea what that meant, so I nodded vaguely.

"Have you ever been electrocuted?" she asked. "Maybe touched a bare wire by accident?"

"Yes. Once I grabbed an electric-fence wire," I said. "Pow!"

Gemma leaned toward me, her face full of glee. "Do you feel like you've grabbed hold of an electric fence just now?"

116

Chapter 13

"I guess so. It's that tingly, nervous-energy feeling," I said.

She leaned back in her seat, nodding slowly and grinning. She knew what I was talking about. She'd been there. We'd both been there.

Suddenly it seemed like we'd gone on a trip together somewhere. Like we'd made a risky border crossing, popped over into some foreign land, and had made it back. We had lived to tell about it.

CHAPTER
14

After that lunch with Gemma, I had tarot on the brain.

In the middle of the day I would find myself staring off into the distance thinking about that upside down angel or thinking about the significance of the five empty cups. I wondered if each cup could stand for a different person I'd lost along the way. The list was made up of my father, my husband, my mother, Peggy's little Sammy boy, and then I wasn't sure who number five would be—unless number five was me. I had lost part of myself with each death around me.

I'd lost my idealism. My innocence. At times it seemed as though I'd lost my love for life. Lost my fight.

That number five could be lots of things.

A part of me really liked the devil as a symbol for Bernard Hunt. That was a good fit. In my book, his name was Belzebub Hunt.

One afternoon I'd driven up to the schoolhouse to check on progress there. And I was standing on the driver's side of my car just gazing off into the ocean's silver horizon line when the contractor, Fowler Hayden, stumped up to me, stubby fists at his sides, "Earth to Merideth," he called out.

I looked up suddenly.

"Where were you?" he asked in his croaky voice. He reached up and fiddled with his hat.

"Whew! I was way out there," I answered.

"Yeah. Hey. I kinda thought you'd like ta come inside and check some of this stuff out," he said.

"Did you finish clearing out that room?" I asked, referring to that doorway and room I'd discovered beyond the pentagram.

"Yeah, yeah. Cleared it all out. Floor's gotta be replaced."

He started walking back toward the schoolhouse's front entrance.

"Did you find anything worth a hoot?" I asked.

"Oh, I don't know," he said. "I didn't look too close. Newspapers, canning jars, a few old record albums and the like," he said. "It's a nice little space back there. I had a look at the plans, and I was thinking; what we might do is turn that whole stage-area into a bedroom . . ."

"Yeah?"

"And that little room, once we've redone the floor, that could become a full-on bathroom. We could even do some built-ins. Closet space, drawers and such, and so on."

"I like that," I said.

"Come over here," he said, taking me to his truck and unfurled the plans across the hood. We spoke at length about creating room, adding fixtures, and new windows.

Finally we went inside, and he was pointing out spots in the ceiling that were going to mean taking the whole roof off. He showed me where a pipe from an old woodstove had once pierced the roof— might be a good spot for a skylight. He said he could bring in a crew and replace the whole roof in just under a week.

"I don't know if I can afford that," I said.

He shook his head, "Now listen, Merideth, you know you're the only person I've ever known who'd go into a project this size without some help? Some family money or a bank loan or something. You're bound and determined to do all this all on your own. And you're a crazy woman to do it. Most people would've borrowed every cent to do this project."

"I know," I said. "It's just that the less I borrow, the more I get to keep. You know? I'm a tight wad."

He nodded, with a gently mocking smile on his face. "You're gonna need some assistance. That's all. That's all I'm saying. This place is gonna be a little palace when we're finished with it. I think we're all gonna be real proud of this job. But you're gonna have to humble yourself and make a trip to the bank."

I waved to two of Fowler's hired hands, college boys who'd spent a good share of the day cleaning out what was now officially called "the secret room."

Heaps of junk were scattered across the stage area, and as I approached it all, one of the boys, Joshua, said, "You wanna pick through that really carefully, ma'am, there's still a lot of glass and stuff."

I stood over tumbled masses of books that had turned into bricks of mold; wet, dank-smelling newspaper; old rotted dresses, and women's shoes.

"Did a little research," Fowler said.

"On what?"

"Well, I seen all this stuff, and I was curious who lived here, right?" he wrestled with his hat for a moment. "So I went down to the records office; turns out there was an old woman who lived in this place up through the early sixties—1961, 1962, something like that. Died when she was 103 or some such. Super-old lady. You know what her name was?" he grinned.

"What?"

"Pompidou. Eleanor Pompidou," he said victoriously.

"Well, that makes sense."

"Doesn't it? I'd always heard of this place called the Pompidou property," he said. "But I never knew why. Now I know."

"That explains it."

"I like doing that," he confided, "you know, looking things up in the record books. Reading old newspapers down at the library. Better'n any book you can buy. 'Cause that stuff's real—right?"

"Sure."

"This old Pompidou gal, turns out she was the old school marm from way back. And then when there wasn't a town here no more and there wasn't a school or nothing, she just lived here. There was an outhouse out back, and there was a pump, you know, for her water. I showed you where the stovepipe used to be. And I guess she just liked being here.

"If she ever needed anything, she'd hitch a ride into Green Ash and get her food and her whatever else, and she'd come back up here. Spooky old thing, I guess," he laughed.

"Yeah?"

"Well, sure. She lived up here by her lonesome with a bunch a cats, and she didn't, you know, hang around down in Green Ash much, so 'course people made up stories about her. Called her a hag

Chapter 14

and witch and said she did—I don't know—spooky stuff up here by the light of the moon. Blah, blah, blah. You know how people are."

I said, "Well, I knew the property was held in a trust back East, but I didn't know how that had happened."

"Yeah, well, when the old gal finally died, they tracked down a relative somewhere. Out in New Hampshire, like you said, somewhere back East. The trustee was like a third cousin twice removed or some such. Anyhow, they didn't have any use for the land, wasn't worth much thirty-five or forty years ago, and they just let the place go to pot," he said, and then turned to me with the radiant look of a circus ringmaster, "I am so happy somebody is gonna give this place a little TLC. You know?"

I smiled.

"I'm serious," Fowler said. "I hate it when great old historical places like this are just left to rot into the ground. I guess if I'd bothered going to college, I'd be a history professor now."

"But you wouldn't be having this much fun," I said.

We both stared up into the old rafters and listened to the silky breeze squeezing through the golden holes in the roof. In that instant, being in that broken-down schoolhouse was more sacred than being in any of the cathedrals of Europe.

"You know, I think you're right," he said with awe in his voice. "This is probably the best life."

His head gave a short nod as though he'd made an important decision. Then he motioned to the two boys, and they set off outside to pull some things out of Fowler's truck.

I bent over a pile of garbagey geegaws and whatzihooeys. Gingerly I began to pull apart *Life* magazines glued together with moisture and smelly mildew. Within minutes of groping around, I found a cracked pair of reading glasses, chipped tea cups, old black phonograph records as thick as dinner plates, and novels whose soggy covers fell off the moment I picked them up.

Lots of broken glass jars and empty boxes of Boraxo and small cookieless cookie tins and rusted thin, vacant cans of vegetables and sardines and cat food told me that the last tenant had used that secret room as her trash dump.

There was a strange excitement going through someone's forty-year-old garbage. Something deliciously tasteless about it. If Peggy, or even Brenda Ann, knew what a brazen thrill I was getting out of this, they'd cringe. They'd denounce me for the hillbilly heathen that I am.

A few things I began to set aside. A few stained, but dainty, hand-made doilies. A nice wooden picture frame. And underneath what appeared to be disintegrating pillowcases, I found a tin box that once held lemon drops; and when I pried the lid open, I found a small stack of old photographs.

To my sheer delight, in one of the pictures—though badly faded—I could make out a collection of youngsters in two rows. And behind them was the schoolhouse in its early days. Down in one corner someone had penned "1906."

The kids in the photo were solemn. Their ages appeared to go from about eight or nine years old up to late teens. Some of the boys wore overalls, and others wore loose shirts and pants with suspenders. The girls wore plain, shapeless dresses. This had been, after all, a mining town where no one made much money. At one end of the group, I could see the bleached-out figure of an adult woman. Presumably the school's teacher.

I felt like an archeologist breaking into King Tut's tomb.

When Fowler and the boys were back inside, I called them over, and we all spent a few moments "ooohing" and "awwing" over the photos.

"I bet the paper might want to print these things," Fowler said.

One of the boys had gotten into the spirit now. He pulled a long, flat wooden box out of the rubble and brushed off damp crumbs of cardboard and crud. There was a little metal clasp at the front of the box, which he flipped up, and we crowded around as he lifted the lid.

Inside, the box was lined in red felt that was falling away. The fabric was moth-eaten and water-stained. Inside was a wooden panel of some sort that he gently, gently tugged out and turned over.

It was a curious thing, like a board game, painted with rows of letters of the alphabet and Egyptian, occult-type images. At the top in the center was a magician wearing a turban, and there were pyramids and palm trees here and there. Over the head of the magician were painted the words, "Magical Talking Board."

"Oh, my ..." Fowler breathed. He patted his stout chest anxiously.

"What is it?" I asked.

"It's a Ouija board," he said. "I never seen one like this before."

The two college boys exchanged a worried glance.

"Really?" said one of them.

Then the three of them looked at me.

"Oh, boy. That's a little ... that's a little weird," I said. "Don't you think?"

Fowler reached into the box and pulled out a triangular thing. "This is what they call the planchette."

"What's that for?" I asked.

The boys both laughed nervously. We were all feeling jittery.

"It's, uh, it's what your spirit guide uses to point out letters and spell messages and so forth," he said, licking his thick lips. "You put your fingers on it and it moves."

"It moves on its own?" I asked, recoiling from the thing.

"Well ... people have different opinions," he said. "But ... I won't touch them. I've heard too many stories."

"Yeah," one of the boys, whose face had grown flush, said, "I knew this girl who, like, when she was using a Ouija board, she went crazy. I mean, I guess a voice came out of the board and, man, she went totally, totally psycho. Like overnight."

"You knew her?" I asked him.

"Yeah. Well, yeah. Actually I knew her sister, but ... it was weird," he said, flustered.

Fowler's face was close to the board. "Wow, I never in my life seen one quite like this. This is old. This is pre-Parker Brothers."

"You've seen one of these before?" I asked him.

"Not this one, this one's really dated. But sure, yeah, I saw one back in high school. You know, at one of those late night party deals," he said. "Won't touch 'em myself."

The boy holding the board thrust it toward his young friend—who immediately held up his hands. "Hey, I don't want it," he said, laughing awkwardly.

And so the board was shoved in my direction.

I didn't know what else to do. I shouldn't have done it ... but I took it.

And I got that electric-fence feeling again. All through me, as though my nerves had all become hot electrical lines. Humming and buzzing throughout my whole body.

I took the antique Ouija board in my hands. And we all looked at each other as if to say "What now?"

CHAPTER
15

"What were you thinking?" Marc demanded.

I looked at my towering nephew, and I despised him more than words can describe.

Marc was up from Los Angeles for a few days. And we were all at Peggy's house having dinner on a warm Sunday night.

He'd been lording over everyone how he'd gotten this role on that TV soap opera. And about all the supposedly famous people he knew. Of course, his angle was, he was going to make it big in Hollywood and then set out to win everyone there over to the Lord.

"Hey, if they embrace Christianity like they've embraced Scientology, then you'll see a big difference in the way TV shows are made," he'd said. He boomed on about the Christian theater group that he was running. Actually, on closer questioning from Brenda Ann, it turned out he wasn't running it; he was sort of coordinating some aspect of it that he didn't go into. And, actually, they hadn't ever performed anything, nor were they rehearsing anything. They were working on script ideas.

The upshot was they were hanging out at someone's apartment, eating pizza and shooting the breeze every other Thursday. This is what Marc's Christian theater group was all about. When you got right down to it.

Then Brenda Ann wanted to really ruffle things up. She pulled her middle child routine and told everyone the story she'd promised not to tell. She told them all in exaggerated detail about going up to the schoolhouse with me and finding that pentagram and all the chicken remains and the altar-to-Satan stuff scattered around. She made it sound like I'd just become the owner of the devil's guesthouse or something.

"And this is the place you just bought?" Marc shrilled. If he'd lived 600 years ago, he could have been a grand inquisitor and I could have been a heretic.

"Yes, I bought the place. So what?" I retorted. "It's just a nice old schoolhouse."

"Are you going to have an exorcism?" he said.

"A what!"

"Are you going to have the place cleared of demons?" he wanted to know. "Because let me tell you, once the devil has made his home there, there's no chance he's just going to move on. There's holy ground, and there's unholy ground, and you've got to decide what's it going to be," he said. "I talked with a missionary from Ghana one time, and he was telling me how many, many times he had to free a home of evil spirits."

As he nattered on, my brain stopped listening to him, and I looked at this male creature who was the product of my sister's loins.

Marc had shown up that afternoon wearing black sunglasses; a white, shiny suit jacket; and slacks. No socks. His black, curly hair was mineral-oiled back across his vast skull. He wore a tie covered in tropical birds. Marc was an actor, and he was a male model, and he was widely considered to be quite handsome; but the fact is, he looked like the owner of a cheap Miami discotheque.

Peggy looked worried. "Merideth," she said in a warning voice. "I didn't know about this." Then she glanced at Brenda Ann and back to me. There was enough reproach in her eyes for both of us. "What've you two been up to?"

"Nothing," Brenda Ann said. "I'm not up to nothing. I won't go back out there."

I sighed. "It was just something some kids were up to, Peggy," I said. "It's no big thing, I cleaned it all up. It's gone."

Marc shook his head. "Aunt Merideth, you can't take this stuff lightly. The devil looks like a lamb, but he's a wolf underneath. A sheep in wolf's clothing."

"You mean a wolf in sheep's clothing," I corrected.

"Whatever," he snapped. "I'm serious here. This is a life or death thing. The devil was a being of light who fell from heaven and took a third of the angels—"

"Yes, I know all about the devil," I interrupted. "It's not like the place is some kind of shrine to devil worship or anything. It's a schoolhouse. At one time it was even a church, as far as anyone can tell."

I had no doubts as to what these three would say if I told them about the Ouija board.

"You should have a pastor go up and pray over the place, have a rededication service," Marc said.

"It's not a bad idea," Peggy said.

"And if it was a church, then it was a house of God. No wonder the devil wanted to defile it. You should have it rededicated. I'm totally serious," he said. "I'll do it myself if you won't," he said.

Peggy nodded. "Listen to what he's saying."

"I hear what he's saying," I said, trying to keep my patience. "And I appreciate your concern, but please."

"I could—" he started in.

"Marc." I held up my hand for silence. "Enough. You made your point."

The meal continued without conversation for some time. Every now and then Marc would try to catch my eye, so I could further witness his disapproval. But as far as I was concerned, it was "case closed."

It was quite a portrait we made there at that supper table. Braden was banging away in his high chair, his mouth crazily lip-sticked with tomato sauce, while Peggy was hovering over her plate, carefully picking at her food with a fork. Her white hair looked like a cloud floating over a small kingdom. Marc was on one side of her, still in that suit and that ridiculous tie, his hair perfectly oiled in place. On Peggy's other side sat Brenda Ann with her mop of hair, wearing a dingy hemp necklace and the ever-present nose ring. Each so different and yet so alike in that way of families who've been through too much.

We all stay sane in our own way.

Later that evening as I was preparing to leave, Brenda Ann and I were upstairs putting little Braden into his crib. He was lying on his back, with his little naked feet in the air, his head weaving slowly side to side, making sleepy, happy sounds as I rubbed his tummy.

"You should listen to Marc," Brenda Ann said.

"Come on," I protested.

Chapter 15

"I know he's a pain," she said, "but I think he has a point. I know about this kind of stuff. I told you about those kids I hung around with up at Humbolt. That one guy Donovan could read your mind. He had some kind of satanic power. It's real, and I don't want to see you get into something freaky. Stuff like that can get way freaky."

"Brenda Ann—look at me. I'm almost fifty years old. I don't know a pentagram from a hole in the wall. What do you think is going to happen?"

"I don't know," she said, worried.

"Do you really think if I move into that place that somehow, someway, the devil's gonna get me? I mean, do you really think it's all that powerful and pervasive?"

She nodded. "I know that weird stuff happens. I just want you to be OK. I . . ." She shook her head and looked down at her child. "Ever since this little guy came into my life, I've thought about things differently. I've thought about, like, what am I going to teach him to believe in? You know? What kind of example am I gonna be to him? I've started thinking pretty seriously about . . . what I hope he'll be when he grows up."

I gave her a hug, and she felt small and sad in my arms.

Brenda Ann's voice got tiny and quivery. "I just . . . I think about Sammy . . . you know? Little Sammy Boy . . . he was so young and so sweet . . . and grandpa and . . . Uncle Simon . . . and you. I want us all to be together again someday. You know what I mean?"

I nodded. "Yeah," I whispered.

"That's big-time stuff," she said. "I mean, I've never been all churchy and everything. But, lately . . ." She shook her head in a kind of exasperation. She was desperate with large questions. "Maybe that's what I need. You know? A church. Maybe that's what Brady needs. Maybe there's something to what Marc has and what Mom has. I mean, look at Marc—he's so sure of every-thing."

"He's cocky," I said.

"Right, I know, he's cocky. But he's that way 'cause he knows what he's talking about. I mean, he doesn't struggle with stuff. With faith and with who God is and how you're supposed to live your life. He doesn't mess around. Everything is black and white with him. And with Mom? Maybe it's not so black and

127

white with her, but she has . . . she has calmness. She has peace."
She looked lost and downcast. "I want that. I want . . . I just want
to know. I don't want to . . . have so many unknowns. I don't want
to be afraid of the future."

"You're not afraid of the future."

She pulled away and looked up at me. Very directly. "I am." Her
mouth bunched up in a determined way. "I am. I just figured that
out. That's why I've gotten into all this protesting about cutting down
forests and about oil companies and the coastline. I'm afraid of the
future."

I watched Braden. He was asleep now, and his tiny human perfec-
tion was startling. The perfect shape of his miniature nostrils and
his small rose-colored lips. I ran a finger across his face, tracing the
roundness of his cheeks.

"I'm not sure those questions ever go away," I said. "Even if you're
Marc. I think he just hides it better."

Brenda Ann began to walk toward the door and then turned back
to me. "Just be careful, OK?"

"OK. Of course."

"I love you," she said.

"I love you too, hon."

CHAPTER
16

That night I went back to my temporary one-room apartment at Green Ash Gardens. In the darkness as I got out of my car, I could smell the redwood trees all around the house. I let myself in and didn't bother turning on the lights. I was worn out, and yet the idea of sleep wasn't quite there for me.

I kicked off my shoes and sat on the edge of the bed.

A trickle of bone-colored light came in through the six-paned window, and as my eyes adjusted, the room became a stark scene of whitish shapes and deep shadows. All the colors of an X-ray.

Over on the coffee table, I saw that old Ouija board. I'd brought it home, had taken it out of its flat box, and cleaned it off several days previous. Its smooth lacquered surface glowed in the moonlight.

I was thinking about Brenda Ann and the surprisingly thoughtful woman she was becoming. Her newest round of life questions had struck something deep inside me. Questions about the world we can see and the world we cannot.

It's funny. I'd had all those questions at one time too . . . such a long, weary time ago. Had I ever gotten answers for them? Or had I just gotten worn-out from wrestling around with them . . . going around and around like a hamster in a wheel . . . and stopped asking them?

I stared at the Ouija board. I didn't want to step onto dangerous ground. But it was time to ask questions again. Time to find things out for myself.

I wasn't an atheist. Far from it. I talked to a God.

A God. A concept that put a distance between me and an actual, living Creator.

I had been so hurt by loving. Loving God. Loving people. Everything I ever allowed myself to love had either died or was taken away.

As a child I had pictured God as a father. That was easy. I was really picturing my Poppie. It was easy to see God as wise and all-knowing, loving, and considerate. But when my Poppie died, it suddenly, alarmingly, seemed as though God might be just as mortal. Just as impermanent, just as likely to leave a wound that could never quite heal.

I moved over to the Ouija board, and I felt my pulse quicken. Even in this pale light I could make out the strangely crafted numbers across the top. The *Yes* and the *No* each in their upper corners, the words *Hello* and *Goodbye* in separate lower corners. The double row of letters in the center, *A* through *Z.*

I could smell its age. The board was made of wood, oak probably, and the letters and numbers were beautifully painted on. In the center was the face of an Egyptian magician. He had dark occult features and a long, sharp nose.

That quickening in my heart rate, that catch in my breath, the terrified tingle in my hands and feet—where did that come from?

I'd been taught that to touch this was wrong. It meant taking a big, stupid risk; it meant reaching out to touch evil, inviting an evil spirit into the room. Into your very body. Like Marc, I'd grown up hearing stories of missionaries casting demons out of froth-mouthed girls.

But I'd been taught that tarot cards were dangerous too. Even now I got nervous and "freaky," as Brenda Ann would say, thinking about tarot. But was it really wrong? Gemma used an angel deck. Weren't angels God's beings of light?

I remembered that old painting that hung, even at that moment, over my father's desk. It showed the tremendous tide of golden beings who moved between the world we can see and the world we cannot.

And the tarot reading had thrown new light onto my past, present, and future. It had been right-on in its depiction of my life. It had

Chapter 16

touched me. It brought tears down my cheeks. It had given me courage for the future. Should I turn my back on tarot cards just because I'd been told to do so?

I supposed the real question was this: How did the tarot cards know all that about me? Who was operating them? Who was directing them?

Gemma said it was angels. And I had decided that it was angels too, but there was still a frightened wanting-to-hightail-it reaction in my stomach—a superstitious part of me, maybe, or a scared "little woman" part that wanted to run from shadows.

To whom do you listen?

As I lay in my bed, I found myself pulling the covers way up to my face. I was afraid of that Ouija board. I was panicky about having it in my house.

My heart would not stop pounding.

I couldn't sleep, and I turned and twisted. I kept hearing noises, and my whole body would flinch. Finally I got up and walked around the room. I turned on the light and peered squinty-eyed all around the apartment, trying to convince myself that I wasn't being overtaken by evil forces.

Everything was fine. Of course it was fine. And I turned off the light and climbed back into bed. Then I sat up and stared at the Ouija board, hoping that by looking at it I could convince that frightened part of me that it was just a piece of wood with letters and numbers on in.

After what seemed like hours, sleep was coming in little drifting moments. But it was always shallow, and I felt like I was toiling for each precious moment of unconsciousness.

Finally at three in the morning, I realized I was angry. Angry that I was afraid of the Ouija board.

I was no "little" woman. I was no frantic baby bird. I was practically menopausal, for Pete's sake. I had seen lots of life, I had run up against all sorts of scary doorways, and I had walked through them.

And if I had learned anything, I had learned that if I was afraid of something, that meant it was conquering me.

And I wasn't going to let that happen.

CHAPTER
17

Gemma bent over the Ouija board with a small smile in her face. "This is a beautiful antique," she said.

"I know."

"Merideth, this is so . . ." She took in a breath, running her hands over the surface, fingering the numbers and letters. *"Mmmm . . .* This is all hand-painted." She looked closer and then moved her head, getting a different angle. "Did you see this?" She bent over the figure of the magician in the center. "Did you see his eyes? They're little colored stones. Glass, probably, huh?"

Now I bent closer. "Sure enough. Well, I'll be—little red pieces of glass. You think that's glass?"

"Probably. I'm no expert, but I'd be pretty surprised if they were rubies or something semiprecious. Still. Still! This is a one-of-a-kind. It really is."

"Do you think it's worth anything?"

"Absolutely it is," she said. "Do you ever watch that show on PBS, 'Antiques Roadshow?' "

"No."

"People bring things on, and they have antiques appraisers who tell them what their things are worth—usually it's things like old lamps and dressers. It's a lot of fun. And goodness—Ouija boards and occult collectibles are very big right now. Oh, would you just look at this . . ." Her face filled with a glow.

Chapter 17

Gemma's house was not the mansion that I'd expected. She lived on her own in a tidy two-bedroom home on a pretty tree-lined street in Green Ash. She'd been divorced three times and said she just preferred to be her own roommate these days.

The house had lots of built-in shelves and coves that she'd filled with books and mementos, chiming clocks and pictures of friends and family. The walls were covered with big paintings in bright colors, and there were rugs everywhere on the hardwood floors. Angels were everywhere too. There were books about angels, postcards with angels on them were taped to mirrors, her refrigerator had angel magnets, angels were stenciled in gold around the walls of her kitchen, and there were angel-shaped candles. She had angels on her coffee mugs.

She even had a big, friendly orange cat named Gabriel.

The living-room windows allowed in thick shafts of afternoon sunlight. Everything was dusty gold.

Gabriel stretched his tubby self out on my lap and gave a rich, welcoming purr.

"Oh, Gabriel," Gemma sighed, "He loves attention of any kind. But you can brush him off if—"

"No, he's fine."

She turned her attention back to the board. "So you were saying you found this?"

I nodded. "Yeah. I found a room that had been sealed off—it was your classic secret room."

"Really!" she said, clasping her hands together, thrilled.

I took a moment to tell her about finding the pentagram and scraping it off and underneath the layer of wet plaster finding the doorway. It took some telling, because Gemma was so deliciously interested in all the details.

"And inside," I said, "once I'd busted through all the plaster and everything, there was all kinds a junk and whatnot. Broken glass, everything you can imagine. And in with all that stuff—I found this thing."

"Wow, oh wow," Gemma said, smiling, "It's just so beautiful..."

She looked at the board and ran her hand across it, gently, thoughtfully, her skin making a dry hissing across the surface. She did this for some time, her excitement fading and her mouth slowly going tight, rigid. Her hand brushing the surface back and forth, back and forth...

Be My Angel

"This is a very powerful one, very old and very powerful," she said, in a dreamy voice. A voice of warning. "You know that, don't you? Can you feel it?"

"I don't know what you mean," I said, shoving my hands underneath my lap.

Gemma looked up, eyebrows raised. "Sure you do. You can feel the power in this old beauty," she smiled in an almost regretful way that seemed to say "You want to think I'm a kook."

She was used to being thought of as a nutball. That was obvious in her expression, her tired smile, her closed mouth, waiting for me to be forthright with her.

"Well...honestly, I've had a hard time with it in the house. It kept me up most of last night," I admitted.

"Yeah..." she said quietly, appreciative of my reply. Now we were speaking the same language. "I mean, it's beautiful, it's lovely workmanship. But you know what I mean then—it's...powerful. You'd really have to know what you were doing if you were using this thing."

I felt that leap in my stomach.

"What do you m—" I kind of choked and put my hand to my mouth. "Excuse me. What do you mean?"

"You have to be careful with Ouija boards. You don't always know who you're contacting."

"Really."

"Sure. I mean there're all kinds of entities out there. And a Ouija board is kind of like a chat room on the Internet. Have you ever done one of those?"

"No. I'm not on the Internet."

"Well, you type in a greeting, and anyone else in the 'room' can answer back. Anyone. You don't know who you're really getting. You can get someone who describes themselves as a twelve-year-old girl from Minnesota, and it's really a seventy-year-old man in a nursing home."

"You don't say."

"Oh, sure. You have to have your guard up. It's the same with a Ouija board. Especially one like this. You can get in touch with some very...mischievous entities. You can get some good ones. Or some...very dark ones."

"I don't like the sound of that," I said.

"No, of course not. I remember when I was a girl . . . This takes me back . . . We had a party at a friend's house. It was her family's cabin way out in the woods. We were miles from anywhere. And it was at night, and one of us had a Ouija board, and we started fooling around with it. We took turns, two girls at a time. And the thing starting working right away. The planchette whizzing across the board spelling out names and messages.

"Well, we got in touch with a spirit who said he'd been a prisoner in life. And we asked what he'd been in prison for, and he spelled out M-U-R-D-E-R. And we were really afraid. I wanted to stop, and so did some of the other girls. But there was one girl, her name was Charlotte Vandershoot. I'll never forget her. She asked the board, she asked the spirit, if he was a good spirit or a bad one, because she said she wanted to get in touch with a bad spirit. She thought this'd be real funny. And the rest of us were saying, 'No, don't ask that!' One of Charlotte's friends started crying. Well, as soon as Charlotte asked her question—zing—that planchette shot across the room into the fireplace and, of course, we all just screamed."

"Oh, my . . ."

Gemma held up a hand. "Next thing then, the whole board started to lift up off the table."

My hand went to my mouth. I felt sick. "What'd you do?"

"Now even Charlotte was scared. We were scared out of our wits. What could we do? We got away from the board, but it floated—it floated on its own—for ten or fifteen minutes. And when one of the girl's mothers got back from town, we BEGGED her to take us home." Gemma's face was somber. "It still gives me chills."

"Oh, my goodness . . ." was all I could say. "My goodness."

"So, like I say, you have to know what you're doing in any case. But with a powerful old board like this . . . makes you wonder what that old woman was up to. What was her name?"

"Pompidou. Eleanor Pompidou."

"She must have been into this pretty deep," Gemma said.

I was so overtaken by panic. And yet I swallowed against it. Swallowed hard. Trying to push it back down. My fists clenching and unclenching.

"Gemma," I said evenly, taking care with my words, "Do I want this thing in my house?"

She considered the question for a moment. "Well, it's not a bad thing, a scary thing, in and of itself. You just don't want to use it without knowing what you're doing."

"I remember hearing that there's a demon with every board. Assigned to every board."

"Where'd you hear that?"

I shrugged. "I don't remember, just something I heard a long time ago."

She nodded. "Well, I don't buy into that kind of thinking. But let's say you were to use this board. There are ways of protecting yourself."

"Like what?"

"Well, more advanced practitioners can learn to call on the white light. You can draw a protection circle around yourself."

I collapsed back into the couch. Calling on the white light? This was beyond all. "I can't do this," I said. "I can't play these kinds of games. This isn't my thing, Gemma . . ."

"You're afraid of it," she said, staring at me.

I nodded in an exaggerated way. "Yes, I am." I laughed in a hee-haw, nervous-nelly way. "I'm not proud—it kinda scares me."

"Well, then . . ." she smiled at me sweetly, "Merideth, what's your interest in it?"

"In this?" I laughed, nodding at the board. "Oh, I don't know. It's just a curiosity. You know? Hey, there it was, in with all that junk."

Gemma nodded. A mysterious smile on her face.

"What's that smile for?" I asked.

Her head bobbed side to side in a jovial, considering-how-to-say-what-she-was-going-to-say way.

"Well, think about it," she said. "It's like Alice in Wonderland, she went down a rabbit hole, and you went through a pentagram."

"Gemma . . ." I shook my head.

"Think about it. You went through a pentagram, and on the other side of the pentagram you found a doorway. A doorway to a dark, secret place of mystery. And in that dark place . . . there you found—this. A Ouija board. I don't think that's coincidence. Do you?"

I looked down at Gabriel still in my lap. "No."

"But that's not all of it. That's just the story of how you were drawn to it. Or maybe I should say, how it called to you."

A tight spot formed in my head. Like my brains were being wrapped into iron knots.

Chapter 17

"Gemma," I whispered, chastising her for thinking that way. For saying such a thing.

"It called you," she insisted, "because you called to it. That's how energy travels. Whether you want to admit it or not, you wanted to find this thing. Power attracts power. You sent out a powerful call, and this is what answered to you. Think about it, Merideth. Think about it seriously."

I nodded. With delirious panic.

There was a long silence in which I could almost hear the sun sliding down past the rim of the earth. The gold in the room was turning to rust and amber.

I took a breath, held it. Held it. Held it. And slowly, in the longest exhale of my life . . . let it out . . .

"I. Have. Questions," I said.

Gemma nodded without speaking.

"I still think about the people who're gone . . . I think about my husband. I still . . . I still feel so badly about . . ." I put my hand to my mouth to cover my quivering lips. I choked out the words. "I killed him . . . and . . ."

Gemma moved closer, her hand stroking my back. Her voice was kind. "Oh, honey . . . oh, honey . . ."

My face was in my hands, and my hands were puddling up with tears. "I . . . had them pull the plug on him . . ."

There was a kick and a kick and a kick deep inside me, and a wall broke open, and I sobbed out huge, open tears. There for a minute, I got a terrible feeling that I'd never be able to stop. I was sobbing and trying to talk, and through it all I heard Gemma's calm, gentle voice, "It's OK . . . it's OK."

After some time I sank back on the couch, and Gemma handed me a little box of tissues, and I mopped up my eyes and my face and my neck and my hands and arms. Tears were everywhere.

Then I looked down, and I saw that fat, old Gabriel was still in my lap. I started laughing at the silly tub still comfortable as the emperor of China in the middle of all my boo-hooing.

"He hasn't moved," I laughed.

"He's seen plenty of tears in his day," she said. "He doesn't know the difference anymore between laughing and crying."

I let out a big sigh. "Oh, I'm so sorry, Gemma—"

"No—"

"I've really made a mess of things here, and I just—"

"Please, Merideth."

"Blubbering away here like a baby, I'm just real sorry."

Gemma shook her head. "Don't be sorry about the way you feel. Don't apologize to me for crying."

"But I lost control."

"Good."

I shook my head. "I hate crying . . . My mother used to cry at the drop of a hat, and it always seemed so . . . To me she was the picture of the 'little woman.' I mean, that's not being completely fair, but I always felt so bad for my dad having to put up with all that feminine weepiness."

"Did your father ever complain about it?"

I thought about it for a moment. "No. I guess he didn't."

"If he didn't care, why should you?"

"Because it seemed so silly. It got on my nerves, you know?"

Gemma gave a lovable chuckle. She was a good person to talk to. She didn't mind my little quirks and clodding, plodding loudness. Maybe she was a little lonely, too, living in that tidy cottage with herself and her cat and her memories of three marriages come and gone. I don't know what it was, but we clicked. Her New-Agey stuff gave me the heebie-jeebies just a little. But she was such a sweet person; her viewpoints and little philosophical asides kind of made me see things in a new way.

She pulled some iced chamomile tea out of the fridge, and we just talked and talked. The sky slowly changed from orange to purple twilight. And twilight sunk away and became night.

Finally our conversation came full circle, as these things often do.

Gemma had moved to a wicker chair across from the coffee table. A lamp was on in the next room, and she'd lighted some angel-shaped candles. She pulled her legs underneath her and said to me, "What was that you said about your husband earlier? Is it OK for me to ask?"

"That poor man," I said. I could talk about it now. "He was in the worst accident you can imagine."

"A car accident?"

"Out on Highway 1. A truck hit him, knocked him off the road, down a ravine, and it's a spot where the road makes a hairpin, so he landed back on the highway below, and a Jeep hit him."

Chapter 17

"Oh, that's awful."

"I got the call and rushed down to the hospital and . . . They managed to keep him alive. In fact he was alive, in a coma, for a year. They moved him down to Oakland at first and then over to the hospital in Ukiah, and they kept him going with a respirator and a feeding tube and all the technology they have now. And I have to tell you, I couldn't stand to see him like that. He'd worked on a fishing boat, he'd been a painter, he wrote music . . . And he just kind of became this . . . thing. This thing in a hospital in Ukiah. I felt so guilty about thinking of him that way, and I kept reminding myself that it was him, it was Simon. That was my man. But he just kept looking like a corpse whose chest moved up and down. And there was a part of my brain that just shouted, 'Why won't someone let me bury him!' You know?"

Gemma nodded.

"So after about a year of that," I said, "I talked with one of the nurses. Her name was Chile. She knew how much I loved Simon. She'd seen me make the drive to Ukiah five times a week and stay for hours and hours at his bedside. I'd keep him up on all the news, who was getting married and who was having kids and all that. And I'd read to him, and I'd play things on the cassette, you know, music he liked. So I talked to this nurse, and I asked her if there wasn't something that could be done to end all this suffering. And I knew, just by looking at her, that she was gonna do it. It was like she'd been waiting for me to ask, knowing I'd eventually come to that decision and waiting for it. You know?"

Gemma nodded. "I have a doctor friend. They'll do that sometimes, just real quietly. They know when there's nothing else they can do."

"So I knew that she was gonna do it. And I went back to Simon, and I kissed him, and I said good night to him. I wanted to say goodbye; I tried to make those words come out, but I couldn't. I just said good night like I always did, and I ran a comb through his hair so he'd look nice and, I remember, his lips looked dry, so I put on a little Chapstick. And . . ." I shook my head. "I went out to the parking lot, and I just sat in the car and cried a bucket. I knew that was it. And, sure enough, next morning I got the call from the hospital. He'd died in the night."

Gemma glanced down at the Ouija board. Then she looked up at me, her eyes full of questions.

"Yeah, so . . . when I came across this old thing," I indicated the Ouija, "I guess some kind of thought entered my brain. I've always thought that, well, if people die and they really do pass on to somewhere else . . . if they kinda head off on some Yellow Brick Road . . . seems like there should be some way to bridge the gulf . . ."

Gemma nodded.

I said, "I haven't always believed in souls."

A crinkly, puzzled look came to her face. "Really?"

"No," I shook my head. "My Poppie—my father—he didn't believe in the soul. He said that there's a place in the Bible that says 'The dead know not anything.' And he took that to mean that when we die, we die. Ker-plunk. We drop into the ground and wait for Jesus to come again. And I just took that at face value." I shrugged and smiled, "He was my father. That's what he believed, and I wasn't going to argue with him. But . . . after he died, I had such a vivid dream of him."

"Within three days?" Gemma asked.

"Yes, how'd you know . . ."

"A soul will usually stay present about three days before leaving," she said.

"Well," I said, "It was one of those dreams you have just before waking up, so it seemed very real, and it stayed with me. I remember in the dream I was on the porch of our family home and we'd come back from the funeral. I was still wearing the dress I'd worn to the graveside. And I was sitting in this old Adirondack chair on the porch. And I was so sad, I missed him so badly, and there he came up the driveway. I was so happy and so surprised, and I remember he acted like it was nothing. Just real nonchalant like he always was.

"He looked young and handsome. He was wearing—I can still remember what he was wearing to the last detail—he was wearing his church suit, but it wasn't black. His real church suit was black, but this one was a beautiful white. A beautiful white suit, and he was wearing what I used to call his Bing Crosby hat.

"I remember we talked, and he was sweet and comforting. And then I woke up, and I was sad about waking up. I wanted the dream to be real; I wanted him to be back. So I went through that day and the next and did all the usual stuff—but I couldn't get that dream out of my mind. And then one night I was in bed. And it was late, and to this day I don't believe I was asleep. I was in bed, and I heard slow footsteps come up the hallway. And for some reason, my heart started pounding. And I heard the footsteps stop outside my door . . . And I heard him call my name . . ."

Gemma smiled broadly and gave a teary-eyed squeal of delight.

"No," I said in a scolding voice, "I was scared. Remember, I'd been taught from day one that there are no souls, and anything you hear along that line is from the devil. The devil impersonated the dead . . ."

Her face soured, and she shook her head, "Oh Merideth . . ."

"So there I was hearing this soft voice calling my name . . . called my name three or four times, and I wanted to turn around . . . I wanted to see him. In the dream it hadn't been scary at all, but to actually hear something or someone calling to you from out of the dark of night . . . Gemma, I was shaking so bad you could hear the bedsprings rattle."

"What happened?"

"I just lay there in a sweat, and I clutched the blankets in my fists and prayed for the voice to stop . . . And it did. And for a long time, for years even, I considered that to be a moment where prayer triumphed over Satan but . . . I wonder now . . . I have to wonder . . ."

"Did anything of that nature happen when your husband died?"

I sighed. "His was different. He was in that coma for so long . . . Sure, I had dreams about him. But the one that stayed with me was after he died. I was in such turmoil and heartache over how things ended. I felt so responsible, that I talked to him out loud at home, 'Did I do the right thing?' 'Should I have given it more time?' 'Was I more wrapped up in my own grief than in your health?' "

"Merideth, I think the fact that the nurse was so willing to pull the plug should be an indication to you that medical science felt there was nothing else to do."

"I know, I know, I've told myself that for a long time. Anyway, about three weeks of this soul-searching was going on, and I remember I had a dream about Simon. And it was a funny thing. It's like I was in another world. I can't tell you how I knew that, but it was somewhere else. Not earth. And Simon was there, and he was happy," I smiled and shook my head, "but he was busy. He was a teacher there, and I know he loved me, and there was affection there, but he had a lot going on . . . It was just a brief glimpse. It let me know that he was fine, but I wasn't. I wasn't fine. It never gave me the peace of mind I needed. I just . . ."

"Do you want to contact him?" Gemma asked.

I nodded, slowly, emphatically. "It scares me, though."

"What scares you?"

"I don't know."

Gemma shifted her gaze across the room and then looked back at me. "What would you say?"

"I..." I shook my head, feeling that sting in my eyes again, feeling a plaintive sorrow rise up inside. "I'd want to know if what I did was OK. I've felt so guilty about it, Gemma. Guilty for thinking of him as a thing. And...I've felt like I killed the man. You know? Can you imagine what that's like?"

She shook her head and said 'No' so quietly I couldn't hear her voice.

I sighed. "I think I'm looking for forgiveness. Or ... or to know that it wasn't a bad thing to do. But—but you've got me convinced that I don't want to use this thing." Nodding to the antique board. "So..."

"You don't want to use this, it scares you, and you should stay away from it," she said, "but, I think I have just the thing." She rose from the chair with a grunt and said, "Hang on a sec," heading into another room. She reemerged a moment later with a long, flat box. She sat opposite me and opened the box and unfolded another board. It was similar to my Ouija. It had numbers and letters on it, it had a *Yes* in one corner and a *No* in another, but it had a much different look. Beautiful and celestial. In the center was the figure of a bright, white angel. He had a strong, lovely face turned upward into heavenly light. His broad, strong wings were carrying him up through towers of white clouds.

"What's this?" I asked, dazzled.

"This is an angel board," Gemma said. "Isn't it nice?"

"Yes," I nodded. "It's quite handsome. What do you do with it? It looks kinda like my Ouija board."

"Well, yes," she answered in an explaining voice, "It's like a Ouija board, but it's designed specifically to put you in touch with angels."

"How so?"

"Well, like I said, a regular Ouija board is like an open line to the other world, and you don't know who's going to answer. But the angel board, it just calls to heavenly, white-light beings."

"How do you know?"

Chapter 17

"Well, that's what it says on the box," she laughed. "I just got it, actually. Why don't we try it and see?" Then she stopped short, thinking intently, then looked at me. "Merideth, I have an idea. Let's not make this a big thing. Let's just try out the board, do a couple of quick things, just, you know, to let you dip your toe in, so to speak. Would that be OK?"

I nodded. That sounded safe enough.

She continued, "I just don't want you to do something you're afraid of. And I don't want it to be the be-all-and-end-all of angel board sessions. Where we try to pack in all of life's answers. Let's just ... try it out."

"Suits me."

She grinned, "Really? You're sure?"

I nodded and smiled bravely.

"Off we go," she said.

She took my Ouija board clear into another room; we agreed that neither of us was up to dealing with that one. Then we cleared away a few things on the coffee table and then laid the angel board out. Gemma placed candles around the board, and then she scooted in next to me and placed the planchette on the board. The planchette looked like a coffee table for a Barbie doll. It was arrow-shaped with a leg at each of the three corners. Each of the legs had a felt pad at the bottom which, I learned, made the planchette slide more easily over the board's surface.

When we were all set, Gemma grasped one of my hands and said, "It's a good idea to close your eyes in a moment of meditation."

"OK."

"It helps you concentrate, and it puts your energy in the right places."

I closed my eyes and before I knew it, these words popped into my mind, "Dear Lord, help this to be OK ..."

It struck me odd that I would automatically start praying for help when all I was doing was calling on angels. *That child's prayer stuff runs deep*, I thought. And my mind went into a tailspin, chastising me for being such a fraidy cat of this stuff and trying to stop myself from praying like I had when I was nine.

Then Gemma squeezed my hand. She had finished meditating, and I hadn't even gotten a chance.

"Ready?" she asked.

I nodded.

"OK, do like this," she said, as she showed how to place two index fingers lightly on the planchette.

I did it.

Gemma closed her eyes and a long moment passed . . . We both took deep breaths . . .

When she spoke, it was a soft, supplication. "We're here tonight to get in touch with the white light," she said. "We have no fear . . . We have no questions . . . We just want to feel the presence of angels . . . Is there anyone willing to talk to us . . ."

We waited. My fingers rested on the edge of the planchette. They were shaking.

We waited.

Gemma said again, softly, softly, "Is there anyone who is—"

The planchette moved.

Slowly . . . smoothly . . . gliding across the board . . . I saw it move . . . from the center of the board, across the image of the angel . . .

"Are you doing this?" I whispered to Gemma.

"No!" she answered.

I looked closely, and I could see that her fingers were barely touching the edge of the planchette. At times it moved away from her fingers completely and still pressed so gently, yet so compellingly, against mine . . . sliding into the lower right hand corner . . . slowly, uncertainly at times, but always moving . . . stopping over the word *Hello,* at the bottom of the board.

"Hello!" Gemma whispered to me.

Her eyes were wide open, as shocked as I was.

I couldn't speak. I just stared, trying to take it in. Trying to make my brain believe what it was seeing.

"My fingers are tingling," I croaked out of a dry throat.

"So are mine."

"All the way up the back of my hand . . ."

"To my wrist," Gemma said, completing my thought.

"Have you done this before?" I asked.

"Not since that time in that cabin," she whispered back. "I just got this board a couple weeks ago. I took it out of the plastic yesterday just to look at it."

Our eyes were both transfixed on the planchette in stupefied amazement.

Chapter 17

It had moved. Somehow it needed our fingers, or our energy or something . . . but it had moved. There was an entity outside of us that had moved that triangular-shaped planchette across the board.

The room felt different. I looked at the candles and saw that they seemed to be burning higher. The shadows around the room looked darker. And it felt as though there was someone else with us.

Gemma spoke my thoughts, "Does it feel like we're not alone?"

I couldn't talk. I just looked at her and nodded my head.

"Why are we whispering?" she asked and grinned. Then she stopped grinning. Jittery. That feeling where you can burst into hysterics or weep or feel crazy happiness or crazy fear or just plain crazy.

We pulled the planchette back to the center of the board.

"You ask something," she whispered urgently.

My lips opened, but my mouth was dry as dust. I closed up for a moment, collecting myself.

It was so quiet.

Yet I could still feel that other presence with us. Just as you can feel someone staring at you on a bus, just as you can tell if someone is reading the newspaper over your shoulder.

I wanted to stop.

I hated being afraid.

I took a breath. "Are you an angel?" I asked.

I stared at the planchette, determined not to let it move because I though it should, determined not to nudge it, determined to let it move only because—

It moved.

Just as before, in answer to a spoken question, it made its silent response by guiding the planchette this time to the upper right hand corner, to the word, *yes.*

It rested there.

Gemma took her hands away from it, put them in her lap, and she said, "Well, we know it works."

I nodded. Too stunned to speak.

"Maybe we should just leave it at that for now—"

"No," I snapped. "Let's ask something else."

I wasn't quitting now. We'd gone too far.

"Are you sure?" Gemma asked. She was looking scared.

"Yes."

I moved the planchette back to the center. And Gemma kept her eyes on me. Suddenly I was the powerful one. I watched her watching me out of the corner of my eye.

"I'm fine," I said.

"Are you?"

"Yeah."

"If you're afraid at all—"

"I'm not."

She put her fingers delicately back on the planchette.

"Do you promise you're not doing this?" I said to her.

"I'm not. Not at all."

I nodded. "I'm going to ask something, and I just want you to go along with it. OK?"

She was alarmed. "Don't ask anything scary."

"I won't," I shot back. "My question is this: I'm going to ask it if—"

It moved.

Before I had finished asking the question aloud, it slipped like a fish across the board to the letter R and came to rest. Then it moved again, to the letter O. Stopped for an instant and then swept over to the letter S and made a quick flinch to the letter E. Where it stopped. Stopped dead.

Gemma repeated out loud. "R . . . O . . . S . . . E . . ." Then she looked at me. Bewildered.

My hands went to my face. I held my face for a long time, gripped the bones in my head, until I felt tears trickling down my fingers and across the back of my hands.

"Rose," she said again. "Merideth, what is it?"

I shook my head. "It's real, Gemma. It knows."

"You didn't even finish your question."

I pushed my face deeper into my hands, a thousand emotions crying out in me. My heart felt like a car wreck.

"Merideth . . . it . . . knew . . ."

"I know!" I gasped.

"The board knew what you were going to ask," she said in awe. "What was your question?"

"I—" I wiped my wet face across the back of my hand. "I had a secret name for my husband," I was able to choke out.

"Rose?" she said.

I nodded. "Yeah," rubbing my nose with my knuckles, looking to her with a sad smile. "Yeah. His name was Simon Ambrose

Chapter 17

Rosensinski. And my name for him was Rose. No one's ever known that. Only us. Only he and I. There's not a chance you're doing this," I said. "You couldn't have known the answer."

"Forget the answer," she said. "I didn't even know the question."

I pulled a tissue out of the box nearby. It was soft and rose scented.

"So . . ." she said. "What do you think about this thing?"

"I think it's real."

"Does it seem scary?"

"Yes . . . and no," I said, then decided, "No."

"Do you want to quit?"

"No . . . this thing is real."

"We don't want to go overboard."

"All right, you're right, but I want to ask one more thing."

She was giving me that look again. Like I might take this too far, like her girlhood friend Charlotte. "OK," she said hesitantly.

We put our fingers on the planchette again, and I waited a heartbeat before asking, "Do you know my Rose?"

The planchette came alive and made its soundless journey across the board and came to rest.

"Yes," Gemma said, when it stopped again in the upper right hand corner.

I pulled the planchette back to the center. Ready for more.

"I want to know if he can see me . . ."

"I don't know," she protested weakly.

I struggled against an onrush of so many questions. "But you're right," I said. "Let's not go crazy. I just want to see what all it knows." Then I asked the board, "Do you know my sister?"

This time, instead of sliding up into the corner, it slowly, haltingly moved to the letter P.

"P?" Gemma asked.

"Peggy," I said. "I've been worried about her . . . she's starting to get a little strange in the head."

"You want to see how she's doing?"

"What do you mean?"

"Well, we don't have to just ask yes or no questions. We could see how she's doing."

"OK."

"Try that."

"OK." We touched the planchette, and I addressed the angel, or whoever we were dealing with. "I'm worried about my sister, Peggy. I wonder if you can tell me how she's doing?"

We waited.

The planchette weebled a little and sidled off in one direction. It was like we had a bad connection.

I looked to Gemma.

"Maybe that's too general a question. Maybe try something a little more specific."

I nodded and again I addressed the board. "How is my sister's health?"

As the planchette began to move, I saw the candle flames flicker in unison and grow long and thin.

In fairly quick succession, the planchette picked out the letters P-W-I-L-D-I-; then it slowed and moved to E, where it seemed to stop and then lurched over to the letter T.

Gemma grabbed a pen and some paper nearby and wrote out the message:

PWILDIET

"What's that?" I asked.

Gemma was very intent on the note pad. "I don't know," she said.

"I think it means whoever this is, they can't spell for beans," I laughed.

"No, I think there's a tendency to conserve energy. It feels like it takes a lot of energy to do this."

"Yeah," I nodded. "I feel kind of drained."

"Right, and so maybe to conserve energy, there's no sense in spelling everything out. I think what you have to do is interpret what you get. For example, we already know that P means Peggy."

"Right," I said, the light beginning to dawn.

"So what we start with is Peggy and then the rest."

I looked at the notepad. "Peggy … wild … I-E-T?" I shook my head. "It doesn't make sense."

"An ET is an extra-terrestrial," Gemma said.

"No, that's nonsense too. Peggy Wild I Extra-Terrestrial." Then I saw it slightly differently and snorted a laugh. "Peggy's a wild-eyed extra-terrestrial. Maybe that's what it means."

Gemma wasn't seeing the humor. "Is she into aliens?"

"No," annoyed.

"What would I-E-T mean … International … Educational …"

Chapter 17

"No, no, no," I laughed. "It's clear as day. It didn't spell out wild, it spelled out W-I-L. Like WILL. 'Peggy will diet.' Oh, my . . ." I said in wonderment. "Is that a joke?"

Gemma gave a short, nervous smile.

"Here, let's ask," I said, "Put your fingers back on the thing."

She shook her head, "I think we oughta wrap it up."

"Come on, come on."

"Really," she insisted.

"Just one more time, I promise. I wanna know if this Peggy Will Diet thing is a joke or not."

Finally Gemma put her fingers back on the planchette, and I said to the board, "Was that a joke?"

This time the planchette moved directly to the word *no* in the upper left-hand corner.

"Peggy will diet," I repeated. "Well, I guess we'll just see. I hope she doesn't diet too much. She doesn't have a lot of flab on her bones as it is."

Gemma gave a big sigh. "Merideth, I'm ready to call it quits, this thing's worn me out. Maybe it's the excitement."

I could still feel my hands and fingers warmed and buzzing with the sensation of a foreign energy moving through them. But I also felt the same sense of being drained.

"OK," I said. "You're right. Let's not push it."

Gemma was quick to put the board away and start turning on lights in the room. She went around and snuffed out all the candles.

CHAPTER
18

"Are you worried about something?" I asked Peggy.

"Only my congestion and this stupid cough," she said. She was involved in a project for her church that had her sitting at the kitchen table folding letters and pushing them into envelopes.

"You're not worried about your weight at all."

She looked at me with a slight grimace. "No."

"I guess it was wrong," I murmured.

"What?" she wanted to know.

"Nothing," I said. "Nothing to worry your pretty head about."

CHAPTER
19

A few days later I was out at the schoolhouse again. This time I came prepared. At the hardware store I'd picked up leather gloves, a small hand rake, a metal saw, and a few other odds and ends—all this would let me safely sift through all the trash that'd come out of the secret room.

It was nasty, wet, gritty work. After an hour of tackling this heap of ick, I was making progress, though. I had three piles going.

One was trash. Unreadable, soggy old newspapers. Rotted pieces of cloth. Clumps of rusted, encrusted something-or-other. Trash.

The next pile was my garage sale pile. Empty candy tins. Newspapers and magazines still in decent condition. Blue and green glass bottles. Lantern parts . . . doorknobs . . . a set of records that was a French language course. Who knows, garage sale people will buy anything.

The third pile was, of course, the things I wanted to keep. Like old photos, doilies, letters, and books.

And while this all sounds very practical, what I was really looking for was something else along the lines of that old Ouija board. If Eleanor Pompidou had something that powerful, surely there were other dark secrets tucked away in all this.

I was hooked.

Feeling that planchette's delicate movement against my fingertips . . . feeling it there in my hands . . . seeing it spell out answers.

Offering its Yes and No replies, even giving a formal Hello at the beginning of the session, and signing off with Goodbye.

Feeling that unseen presence. Really feeling it.

How can I describe that?

As a girl I was told about angels, told some of their names, like Gabriel and Michael and a few others. And I heard about seraphim and archangels and the curious, worshipful spirits around God's throne. I heard about celestial hierarchies and angel choirs.

But it wasn't the telling that got me. Not the words. It was the pictures of angels that burned bright in my imagination. My grandfather had a huge, old book of medieval paintings where the angels were odd and angular with their wide staring eyes and their fixed expressions, forever a part of the architecture of vast cathedrals. These for me were the formal, ancient angels.

A friend's family had a book of paintings of later centuries, around the time of Shakespeare and John Milton, who wrote Paradise Lost. These were drama-queen angels. They were slightly chubby, clear-skinned castrati, who were always hanging around in the background when saints were being put to the sword or burned at the stake or filled with arrows. These angels always seemed at a loss as to what to do. They simply cast their eyes skyward, their mouths open with horror, their eyes rolled back in their sockets.

Then, even as a girl, it became clear to me that angels went through a transformation over time. In the paintings of this century and even the last, angels became handsome, athletic looking creatures with male faces. There is a quite famous painting, I think, of two little curly-headed children stooping over a stream. And behind them is an angel who has a flourish of wings and glorious hair and a face of heart-breaking concern.

I've seen illustrations in modern Christian books and magazines of angels as warriors. Rugged-looking guys with long, fashionable manes of blond hair, mouths open in a cry of battle.

It was also the more modern pictures that, once-in-awhile, showed fallen angels. It seemed to be all a part of the "warrior" role that angels had taken on in recent times. Good angels waging war with bad angels.

I would see these images, and in my little mind I imagined what they would really look like. I imagined their world—invisible to us, beings of light who could travel through time and space. In a sense, I made myself believe in them.

Chapter 19

But to stare at that handsome angel in the center of Gemma's board and to speak a question and to feel the planchette move. Nothing could beat that.

Answers were out there.

Those questions that build up over a lifetime—you eventually come to accept that there're some things you'll never really know. And you tell yourself that you have to get used to not knowing.

Faith. That's what you have to work with.

When you don't know what happens after you die, when you don't know how a God of love could create a chamber-of-horrors like this world, when you lie in bed and you've sobbed until you've exhausted yourself and you just want to die and you wonder why you were ever brought in this world, when you beg God to utter one single, solitary word of comfort and the room remains silent—when you've asked so many questions you're sick of asking them—you tell yourself that that's the role of faith.

Faith, you tell yourself, will allow you to gaze prayerfully skyward and say things like, "I don't understand, but I'll trust You."

Though You slay me, yet will I love You.

But with a Ouija board—who needs faith? You ask the questions and—slam, bang—there's someone spelling it out for you.

As I worked and my leather gloves went from new orangey cowhide color to wet, grimy, black, my mind was going through a checklist of things I wanted to ask next time. Now that someone was willing to talk, I had so many questions. Questions they tell you will be finally answered in heaven.

Well, now I didn't have to wait.

CHAPTER
20

"Merideth, this is Nikky," Gemma said in a sugary, introductory voice.

"Hi, Nikky," I said.

"And this is Marty."

"Hi, Marty," I said.

They were a good-looking couple. Nikky was a tiny blonde with an upturned nose. She was probably about twenty-five, but it was sure easy to picture what she must've looked like in first grade. She still had a child's face. And Marty was a big, friendly kid, smiled easily, and had a short brillo pad for a head of hair.

They were both in the Shakespeare Festival with Gemma.

Gemma was playing one of the witches in Macbeth, and Marty was playing a soldier. Nikky was playing Lady Macbeth.

"We just got to telling ghost stories backstage the other night," Gemma told me, as we took seats around her living room, "And I told them about the angel board. They wanted to try it out."

Nikky smiled and gave a laugh that was more like a gasp. "Yeah, I've never done anything like, you know, that. I was just all wondering what it would be about."

"I'm totally into it," Marty said loudly, in grinning anticipation. "I mean, I've never done it, either, but—man—this friend of mine. Robin? He did it all the time. And, the trippiest things happened to that guy."

"Robin was on drugs," Nikky said, giving Marty a grim look.

"Yeah, well," Marty laughed, and shrugged, "Yeah, yeah, I guess he was on drugs." He looked down at his fingernails and then back up with a loopy grin. "He was on a lot of drugs."

Gemma turned to me, "You want some tea?"

"Same as last time," I said.

"You two?" she asked the young couple.

They both nodded politely.

Gemma got up, and I followed her into the kitchen.

"I can tell you're not comfortable with this," Gemma said to me.

"Not really, Gemma," I admitted. "I mean, I have some questions that are ... personal. Some things that I've been thinking about a lot."

Gemma pulled a frosty glass pitcher out of the refrigerator, and I plucked glasses out of a cupboard.

"I thought it would just be you and me," I whispered. "Any other time would be OK, but last time was just testing the waters. Right? I wanted to dig a little deeper this time around."

She nodded.

"I guess I don't see this as being some kind of parlor game you invite the neighbors over for," I said. Hurt. At a loss.

She poured sunny chamomile tea into each glass. "Would you get some ice out of the freezer?"

I rattled out a plastic tray and bent it backward slightly, the ice crackling like knuckles.

"I just got to talking to these kids," Gemma explained softly, "And in a play, you work so closely together ... they're really good kids."

"That's not what I mean," I said. "I'm sure they're nice kids, that's not the point here. The point is, I just didn't expect there to be other people here tonight."

Gemma turned to me. "I'm sorry, Merideth."

She put on that look of longsuffering she was so good at. The look of a martyr on a burning stake. A look of, "what do you want me to do?"

It was almost as bad as dealing with my mother. You can fight anger. You can battle with irritation, and you can whip a smart alec into shape.

What can you do with patience?

I shook my head. "I'm getting old and stuck in my ways," I confessed.

"Yes, you are," she said, and whisked herself out of the kitchen, and I heard her sing, "Here we go."

I waited. And gave myself a short lecture on the art of being human. And I breezed back out into the living room.

There was much talk between the three of them about the goings on backstage at the Shakespeare Festival. From the sound of it, there was lots of coupling. And some uncoupling. Real fights and stage fights. Actors forgetting their lines and forgetting themselves.

The Macbeth story from what I picked up has lots to do with ghosts and witches, apparitions and dark deeds. Sent a tingle up the back of my neck. It's no wonder the angel board came up in that setting.

When it was dark outside, Gemma went around the room and lighted a dozen or so candles, immediately changing the mood of the place.

Suddenly, it felt like a medieval witch's cave.

And just as I had that thought, Gemma started hissing and croaking:

"Double, double
toil and trouble
fire burn and caldron bubble!"

Her face was all twisted up, and she was clawing at the air.

Marty and Nikky laughed, but I sort of shrank up inside. Then I realized she was doing some of her witch lines from the play. And that came as a relief—I thought she was doing some kind of incantation.

Gemma pulled out the angel board, and with the aid of pillows we positioned ourselves around the coffee table.

Marty and Nikky wanted us to start so they could see how it worked.

Gemma and I placed our fingers lightly on that little triangle, and Gemma said a few words like she had last time about approaching without fear and without bad intention, seeking only answers, seeking guidance from the white-light beings.

Then it was quiet.

I noticed chests rising and falling. In Nikky's neck, I could see a large artery pulse-pulse-pulse-pulse quickly against her skin.

Very quiet.

"Is there an angel with us here tonight?" Gemma asked in a low voice.

Chapter 20

Nothing happened, then after a moment, I felt a warmth in my hands.
"Did you feel that?" I asked Gemma.

She looked at me through half-closed eyes and nodded. "Yeah."

"Try again," I whispered.

Gemma made a small *mmmm* sound as though some delicious sensation was coming over her. "Is there an angel with us here tonight?" she asked the darkness and candlelight.

The familiar twitch of the planchette, and it moved as though pulled by an invisible thread to *Hello* in the lower right side of the board.

"Whoa," Marty uttered in awe.

"Oh, wow...oh, wow," Nikky said, her eyes sparkling in the candlelight. "You guys swear you're not doing that?"

"It's not us," I assured her.

Gemma shook her head.

"Do you want to try it?" she asked them.

Marty shook his head. And looked at Nikky.

Nikky said quietly, "Let's watch you guys. Just for a while then . . . we'll try it?" She looked to Marty.

He nodded. "Sure. Sounds good."

"Ask him where he is," Nikky suggested.

"What do you mean?" I asked.

"Well, like, where is this angel?" she said. "Is he in heaven or is he, like, in some other dimension or what?"

"It's a good question," Gemma said.

"Yeah," Nikky said.

Gemma took a deep breath. "One of us here wants to know where you are. Can you tell us where you are?" Gemma asked.

The planchette moved, but it was slow and directionless.

"Try again," I said.

Gemma repeated. "Tell us where you are . . ."

This time the planchette moved with seeming reluctance to the letter O, then to V, and finally, after a feeble effort, came to the letter A.

"What is it?" Marty asked.

Gemma pulled out the same pad of paper we'd used last time and jotted down OVA.

"Isn't that like an egg, like in a mother's, you know, womb or whatever?" Marty said.

"Yeah," I said. "Seems like a strange answer."

"Maybe it's like ova, like over. You know? Like over us."

"Yeah!" Marty cackled. "Kinda sounds like rap. Like, I be ova you," he said.

"I like the idea of the egg, Nikky," Gemma said soberly over the sound of Marty's laughter. "Like the universal egg, you know? Do you know that concept?"

"No," the girl said.

"Do you?" Gemma asked me.

"No."

"Well, it's just the idea that souls are born out of an egg, like a giant spiritual energy source. Like a god-size energy source."

"But if this is an angel, why would he be in a giant egg?" I wanted to know.

"It's not like that," Gemma said.

"I think Marty's right, I think he's ova us," Nikky said.

"Well, you just keep thinking that," I said.

"What's his name?" Marty asked.

Gemma stared at the board for an instant and then looked up at the two kids. "Is he a he?"

A tiny smile came to Marty's face, and a tiny blush came to his cheeks. "Oh, yeah," he said, and rocked back and forth, embarrassed. "Guess it doesn't have to be a he. Could be a she or a something else."

"Ask," Nikky prompted.

Gemma and I curled our fingers and barely-barely touched the planchette.

"We might be asking a foolish question," Gemma said, addressing the air, "But we want to know if you are a he or a she . . ."

The planchette immediately shimmied to the upper left-hand corner. *No.*

"Not a he or a she," Gemma murmured.

I saw Marty and Nikky exchange what they thought was a private glance. Nikky was a little scared, and Marty was trying to good-humor her through this.

We started to pull the planchette back to the center—

It began to move again.

"He's getting lively," Gemma said.

"He's not a he," I said.

The pointer slid over to the letter W and then to the letter E. And stopped.

"We," I said. "What's that mean?"

"Maybe—" Nikky had to clear her throat. She laughed nervously and put her hand to her throat. "Maybe it's trying to tell us what it is."

"How do you mean?" I asked.

"It said it wasn't a he or a she, right? Maybe it's a we . . . ask it that."

This troubled me.

Still, Gemma and I placed our fingertips on the planchette.

She said in a rather small voice, "Are you a—"

Didn't even get the words out. The planchette darted to *Yes*.

"It says it's a we," Gemma said.

"My name is Legion for we are many," Nikky quoted.

I knew immediately what she was talking about, having grown up on the stories of the New and Old Testament.

"What?" Marty asked her.

Gemma cocked her head and looked at Nikky.

"It's, um . . ." the girl's face was red and somber in the candlelight; her voice was shaken. "You know in the Bible?"

"Aw, Nik," Marty groaned loudly.

"I'm serious," she shot back at him. "There's this story about these two men who are possessed with demons. And they come up to Jesus and, uh, I'm kinda fuzzy on the details, but Jesus ends up talking to the demons, and he asks them what their names are. And the one demon says, 'My name is Legion for we are many.' That's all."

She had the uncertain look of nausea.

"Don't get everyone freaked out," Marty said.

"Nikky," Gemma said in a motherly voice, "We didn't ask his— I mean—the angel's name. We asked if it was a he or a she. And it says it's a we. Now, I don't know exactly what that means . . . but can you imagine being an angel and trying to describe to us what it is?" She smiled.

"I don't know," Nikky mumbled.

"Angels, from what I know, are spirits and maybe in some way, they are not individuals. Or maybe they don't think of themselves as individuals. They obviously don't think of themselves as being one sex or another."

"Let's ask its name," Marty suggested.

"You all right with that?" Gemma asked Nikky.

Nikky nodded, but the candlelight glinted and danced at tears in her eyes.

"Do you want to stop?" Gemma asked.

"No," the girl smiled and grimmaced and laughed, wiping at her eyes. "I'm fine," she said. "I don't know why this is—I'm fine. I was raised to think this stuff was, um, well that you shouldn't do this stuff. I don't know why."

"Go ahead," Marty prompted.

We put our fingers on the planchette.

Gemma was again our go-between: "We're having some ups and downs here. We don't really understand your last answer, so maybe this is something we'll be able to understand. Do you have a name?"

The planchette went to *Yes.*

We pulled it back.

"Tell us your name."

The pointer moved first to W then to E.

Nikky took a quick breath. Her head leapt back a little.

And the planchette then moved to the letter X, where it stopped.

"W-E-X," Gemma spelled out.

"That's its name?" I asked. "Wex."

Nikky still looked uneasy. "Does that sound like an angel's name to anyone?" she asked me.

I shrugged.

Marty's eyebrows kept worrying toward each other. "Sounds like the name of a death metal band," he joked softly.

"Yeah," Nikky agreed.

Gemma nudged me, and we put our hands on the planchette again.

"Is your name Wex?" she asked.

Yes, came the reply.

"Are you an angel?" Gemma asked, her mouth set in a look of concern.

Yes, came the reply.

"Ask if it's a good angel or a bad angel," Nikky said.

"What do you mean?" Gemma asked.

"Well—you know," Nikky prompted.

"Oh." Gemma bah-humbugged. "I don't believe in all that clap-trap. This is an angel board. It attracts angels. I don't buy all that Paradise Lost stuff about fallen angels. That's all Christian mythology."

That silenced us all.

"I think I do believe in it," Nikky said.

Gemma was about to lose her cool.

"You two haven't tried this yet," I said. I didn't want an argument. I was tired. Again sensing that "other" energy in my hands and yet feeling like the life was being drained out of me.

"Yeah," Marty replied. "Let's try it."

Nikky looked at the board warily.

"You don't have to if you don't want to," Gemma assured her.

"No, I wanna try it," the young woman said.

We turned the board around, and the two put their fingers on the planchette, and there was some at-length talk about how to do it and how to avoid bumping the planchette yourself and such.

Finally they were ready, and Nikky took a deep breath, and I noticed that all the candle flames in the room stretched slowly and brightened.

Nikky asked, "Are you my guardian angel?"

The planchette didn't budge.

"Are you my guardian angel?" she asked again.

This time the planchette moved, a little unsteadily, to *No*.

They pulled the instrument back to the center of the board. Both were very serious now.

"Do you know my guardian angel?" she asked.

The planchette moved to *Yes*.

"Are you an angel of light or an angel of darkness?" she asked.

Gemma let out an irritated gasp.

All the candles did a jump. So did my stomach.

The planchette made several hesitant moves, and when she felt like she wasn't being answered, Nikky closed her eyes and said in a more commanding voice, "Wex, are you an angel of light or an angel of darkness?"

Now the planchette moved. In a long, grand sweep that started at the center of the board. it made a wide, wide circular motion past the *No*, past the angel's face, making a turn at *Yes*, going past all the letters to—

Goodbye.

There it sat, and we all stared at it for a moment.

"Wex didn't like that question," Nikky said.

CHAPTER
21

It wasn't until months later that I heard what happened when Nikky and Marty left that night.

I ran into Marty in a hardware store, and he asked if I was still doing Ouija board stuff .

"No," I said.

"You mean after that one time?"

"No. I stopped a few days later," I said, and I told him a little of what happened to me afterward. Some of the dark antics that came into my life as a result.

Marty shook his head. "I still get goose bumps when I think about what happened."

Marty told me that that night after doing the angel board at Gemma's place, he had dropped Nikky off at her house, and he'd gone home. Gone straight to bed.

He was uneasy and skittish and didn't want to be in the dark, so he lighted a candle before going to sleep. In the middle of the night, he woke up sweating and thrashing about in his bed from bad dreams. When he opened his eyes, the room was red. As though lighted with a red lamp. And the candle was throwing a large moving shadow on the wall. A shadow that loomed over him like a monster with angry, staring eyes. He felt an oily, watching, predatory spirit in the room. He snuffed out the candle, and the room felt cold. He wasn't alone. There was a spirit with him, something he had invited in through the angel board. A presence with an ill-will.

Marty got up and went to the living room and turned on the lights, where he spent the remainder of the night.

Nikky, meanwhile, had gone to bed uneasily in her parents' basement. And in the darkness and silence of night, she awoke to the sound of a dry, hissing voice whispering, "Wex ... Wex ... Wex ... Wex ..."

She didn't have the strength to leave her bed, and she simply wept, nearly insane and paralyzed with fear, hiding her face under her pillow.

Neither of them was able to talk about their experiences the next day. And finally, a few days later when they did talk about it, they agreed not to say the name Wex out loud.

It seemed like an invitation for a spirit to pass into our world.

CHAPTER
22

Marty and Nikky left soon after Wex sent the planchette to *Goodbye*. They thanked Gemma for the tea and in sort of a uneasy way thanked her for the evening. The atmosphere was strained and strange, and it was a relief to see them go.

Gemma walked them to their car, and I sat in the room with the angel board and the candles. I heard them talking outside over the noise of an idling car engine.

I stared at the board thinking of the name *Wex*. Trying to make myself come up with some kind of meaning for the name. Some connection to something in the Bible or in history or . . . I don't know what.

Although I was weary, my hands were itching to get back on that board. I wondered if you can do an angel board by yourself. Something in me said that wasn't a good idea, but I had long ago given that voice in my head the name of "spoil sport" and "kill joy" and "unadventurous" and sundry other names.

I first put my fingers on one side of the planchette, and I said in a voice that was probably quite small, "Are there any angels with me here tonight?"

I waited for something to happen. I waited. I waited.

Then I tried putting my fingers on both sides.

"Are there any angels here with me tonight?"

Still nothing.

Then I got the idea of placing my fingers along the bottom edge of the triangular planchette.

"Are there any angels here—"

Slowly, slowly it lurched. And moved across the board at half speed. To *Yes.*

I pulled the planchette back to the center.

"Is this Wex?" I asked.

Yes, came the response.

"Are you an angel?"

Yes.

And I'm not sure why I asked this question: "Have you always been an angel?"

This time the planchette teetered over to the word *No.*

I tried the same question, just to be sure, and this time the planchette moved faster to *No.*

Not always an angel. That certainly deviated from the path. I had always been taught that angels had always lived in heaven with God. If Wex wasn't always an angel . . .

"Were you a human?" I asked.

Yes, came the reply.

"Did you die?"

Yes.

"Did you become an angel after you died?"

Yes.

"Did I know you?" I asked, almost too quickly and then became terrified of the response. What if . . .

No, the board replied.

A thrill of relief passed through me. If the response had been *Yes,* I would have fainted.

"I never knew you?" I asked, just to be sure.

No.

I waited. I knew I didn't have much time. I could hear the car starting to back up outside.

"Do you know Simon Ambrose Rosensinski?"

Yes, came a swift answer.

"Can he see me?"

The plachette moved to the letter C and then the letter U. It felt like a question, like, "See you?"

"Yes," I kind of laughed. "Yes, can he see me?"

Chapter 22

The planchette began to move, and then Gemma walked back into the room. She stopped cold. "You're not supposed to do that," she said, a flat, harsh tone. "They say not to do that."

"Do what?"

"You're never supposed to do it alone, they say that's bad."

"It's fine," I said. "He's kind of joking around with me."

Gemma sat across from me, worry, deep worry, in her eyes. "You're going a little fast with this," she said. A little shaken.

"I'm not doing anything different," I said.

She shook her head adamantly. "You're not. Supposed. To do this. Alone."

I rolled my eyes and took my hands away from the board.

"All right," I conceded. "I won't do it alone."

"I don't mean to sound scary. It's just that I want to err on the side of caution," she said.

I nodded. I was really tired now.

"I'm gonna head home," I said. Then I noticed Gemma's face, her eyes were circled in dark wreaths. Maybe it was just the candlelight, but she looked concerned and sallow and uncharacteristically depressed.

"What is it?" I asked.

"Well, just what I said, about going too fast with this? I told you from the onset that I don't do dark, black things. I stick with bright, white-light things. And tonight I felt a foreboding," she said. "I felt superstition, and I felt fear."

I nodded.

"Nikky was looking for something dark and scary here," Gemma said. "She was raised very devoutly, I guess. She was looking for some kind of black-magic show. And I definitely don't want to go in that direction."

I agreed.

"I'm sorry if I scared you," I said, referring to using the board alone.

"No, I'm sorry if I hopped on you. I was still a little psyched out about that fallen angel stuff. I just don't buy that. I just don't. I like things bright and good. You know what I mean?"

I nodded.

"Keep it nice, keep it clean, that's what I say," she said.

I yawned and said I needed to get a move on.

We agreed to meet again soon.

CHAPTER
23

I t was getting to be the end of July, and the Shakespeare Festival was in full swing, so it was difficult to find time for another angel-board session with Gemma.

I wanted one.

I didn't want to scare Gemma, but I was ready to go as far as necessary to get answers. To see where this angel could take me. It still felt like that dream of mine—like I had in some fashion "jumped through the pentagram," and I had entered an in-between place. A place between our world and another world. A world of departed souls and drifting spirits, angels and heavenly beings, demons and fallen angels. This was the biggest thing that had happened to me in a long time. On the phone, Gemma said my psychic door was "opening."

I was reading up on Ouija boards, and I was renting videos on angels, spending time at a little shop in town that sold crystals and tarot cards looking up anything I could on "the beyond."

Everything else came second or third or fourth.

Renovating the schoolhouse.

Looking for a job.

Keeping up with friends.

Spending time with my family.

But that last one wouldn't wait long.

I remember it was late on a Thursday afternoon. It was one of the cold, foggy summer days we get on the coast. I was at home in my

Green Ash Garden apartment straightening books and ironing and tidying up.

I heard the strangest noise. I thought it was a kitten at my front door. There was a tiny, squeaking sound, and I was just going to the door when I heard a very timid knock.

I opened up, and there was Brenda Ann. Her shoulders were hunched, her eyes were red, and her nose was red, and her whole face was wet with tears, and her hair was matted. And she wasn't wearing her nose ring.

The girl just collapsed against me. And then she caught her breath and let out such a sob. Such a heart-breaking sob.

It frightened me.

She was sobbing and trying to talk, and none of it made sense. I dragged her inside and got her on the couch, and I sat down beside her, and she clung to me.

"Mom . . ." she finally got out.

Now I was really scared.

"What, honey? What is it?"

Brenda Ann finally sat back, slowly and painfully, against the arm of the couch and pulled her knees up against her chest. She practiced breathing for a while. Finally she got her crying under control. She was fighting very bravely, so she could say something to me.

After a long time she was finally quiet, her face against her knees.

"What is it, hon?" I asked.

And she just said it: "Mom has cancer."

"Wh . . . what? What did—Peggy had c—"

"She has lung cancer. Can you believe that?"

"No—when did this happen? When did she find out?"

"This morning," Brenda Ann said, digging at her eyes with the heels of her hands. "She has lung cancer. I can't believe it. My mom has lung cancer. This perfect, pristine woman who has never smoked a day in her life, who has breathed this perfect, pristine ocean air all her life, has lung cancer. How does that work? How does that make any sense?"

I felt weak. I barely had the strength to sit upright.

My mind shut off.

I stared at my coffee table unable to say a word. Unable to think a word.

Just stared.

"Aunt Merideth? They're gonna cut out one of her lungs," Brenda

Ann said, leaning toward me. "What if she doesn't make it? People die on operating tables."

"Is that why you took out your nose ring?" I asked in a dull voice. Still staring, still stuck in a weird, numb, blank-gaze, blank-mind state.

"I guess," she said. "I don't want that stupid thing to keep coming between us."

"She hated that thing."

"I know. And it was such a major deal with me. But it doesn't matter anymore."

I took a breath, and I turned to Brenda Ann, and we hugged. We clung to each other. I still couldn't react. It was too much. I just needed to hang onto someone, and I think she needed to hang onto me.

I kept thinking of the message from the angel board: Peggy will diet. Thinking of scrawny cancer patients. People who can't keep down a morsel of food they're so sick from chemo.

"Let's go see your mom," I said.

At the house I found Peggy sitting in bed propped up with pillows. She looked small and tired and sick.

I sat on the edge of the bed, and the bed springs squawked under my weight.

"Peggy..." is all I could manage.

"I've been worried about you," she said in a strong voice. The strength of her voice seemed misplaced in that petite, ill body.

I sat silently and took her small, damp hand in mine. I stroked her hand, looking down at the age-spotted skin over the collection of bones underneath.

I was too overwhelmed to say anything in response. It's like she knew I was doing something in my life that she wouldn't approve of. I was afraid she knew. And I just nodded, admitting, in a wordless, childlike way, that I was up to something bad.

"Can I pray for you?" she asked.

I nodded.

Brenda Ann came to the doorway holding Braden.

"Can I come in?" she asked.

Peggy held out her other hand, and Brenda Ann came in and sat on the other side of the bed.

Peggy's voice was unwavering, clear. "Dear God, dear Father," she prayed, "You have promised to watch over us even in the valley of the shadow of death. We ask now for your watchful care over us.

Chapter 23

We're not big, smart people, Father. We're just us, Your children. Please be with us, gentle Shepherd, and guide us and keep us. Help us to pass through this darkness. Let your love shine as a beacon and guide us to the other side, so that one day we can all be with You and we can say together, Yours is the kingdom and power and the glory forever. Amen."

"Amen," Brenda Ann and I whispered.

"Amen," Peggy repeated.

I took a breath and looked at my sister. She was so calm. So serene. So completely beautiful.

She looked at me and then at Brenda Ann. Peggy kissed her own hand and stroked it onto little Braden's face.

Brenda Ann was crying softly, and I was still too shocked to say anything.

"I have never seen you at a loss for words," Peggy said to me.

I felt a smirk come reluctantly to my face, and then I felt tears begin.

"Oh, Peg," I said, and pressed her hand to my face.

"Oh, please," she said in an imperial tone. "I'm still here. There's no need for a lot of tears. You're embarrassing me."

I felt a tight squeeze on my hand. She coughed. Then she coughed hard and sat forward.

I rubbed her back.

"Are they sure?" I asked her.

"What does an HMO ever really know?" she complained. "They saw a spot on my lung, they biopsied it. It's cancer. The doctor sat me down and was very clear about it all. Sounded like he was reading right out of a handbook. I'm sure there's a handbook on how to tell people they have cancer."

"Brenda Ann said you're going to have a surgery," I said.

Peggy nodded. "Thursday."

"Thursday!" I cried.

"Keep your voice down," Peggy said. "You're always so loud. Why were you always so loud?" she wondered.

"What kind of surgery?" I asked.

"The kind where they take out your lung," she said. "They have a name for it." Then she looked to Brenda Ann, and a mischievous smile snuck up on her face. "Did you notice anything different about our little miss over here?"

I smiled and nodded. Acknowledging the missing nose ring.

"It's still pierced," Brenda Ann said. "I could put it back any time."

"Is this what it's taken?" Peggy asked, in not such a kind voice.

Brenda Ann rolled her reddened eyes. "Mom."

Peggy turned to me abruptly, eyes sparkling. "Did you know that my doctor did this same surgery on John Wayne!"

"So?"

"So"—still weirdly exuberant—"So that's pretty neat, don't you think?"

"Didn't John Wayne die?" Brenda Ann asked, not too pleased.

"Yes," I said.

"Well, he died," Peggy explained, suddenly the expert, "because his doctor made him promise not to smoke cigarettes. He was a terrible smoker. So you know what he did? He started smoking cigars. He started inhaling cigars!"

"You don't even know who John Wayne is," Brenda Ann said. "You don't even watch movies."

Peggy was crestfallen. "Marc would be interested in this. He likes all that Hollywood stuff."

"Did you tell him?" I asked Brenda Ann across the bed.

She blinked and nodded. "Yeah," her soft voice answered, "he's coming up tomorrow."

"I told him he didn't need to," Peggy groaned and coughed.

"He wants to be with you for the surgery," Brenda Ann said.

Braden started fussing, and Brenda Ann said she needed to put him down for a while.

When she was gone, Peggy turned to me. "Where have you been? Nobody's heard a word out of you for a long time."

"I've been busy with the house," I said.

"You can't have been all that busy," Peggy said. "We got a call here from your contractor. He was looking for you."

I shook my head.

"It's been weird not going into work every day. Not having the business anymore," I said.

She nodded. She wasn't convinced.

I couldn't tell her about the angel board. I couldn't. Even if I wasn't convinced that it was wrong, I'd never convince her. She'd never understand. She'd blow a fuse.

"I pray for you," she said softly. "I know you struggle."

"We all struggle," I answered.

"Not like you, Merideth. Not like you. I've just had a feeling lately that you've wandered farther away. I . . . What are you up to?"

"I'm not up to anything," I said, smiling weakly.

"Remember the God of your fathers," she said.

"I know. I remember."

"These aren't just the words of your sister. Brenda Ann worries about you too. Did I tell you that she and Braden went to church?"

"No. But that doesn't surprise me."

"Will you go with her?" she asked. "She could use your support. She relies on you. She looks up to you. You know that, don't you?"

I nodded.

She looked down at the bedspread and smoothed it out over her belly.

"I know I get on your nerves sometimes."

"You don't—"

"I do. I know I do—let me finish. I've never told you this before, but I should. When Poppie was dying, he took me aside. He took me aside, and he asked me to watch out for you. He made me promise that I would watch out for you. To be there for you."

"He did?" I was surprised and a little delighted. I grinned and started to speak, "He—"

She held her hand up for silence. "He wanted to make sure that he saw you again."

Peggy looked at me intently.

"You have," I said. She seemed to need to know that.

Peggy nodded. "I love you, Merideth. I'm your sister."

Neither of us spoke for some time.

"Answer me this," I said. "Are you gonna be OK?"

"I don't know."

"Do you care?"

"Of course, I care. No one wants to get sick, no one wants to die," she said.

"It doesn't seem like you care much. Don't you want to know? Don't you want answers to things like that? Don't you want to know if you'll live? Don't you want to know what happens—let's say you don't make it, Peg—don't you want to know what happens if you die?"

"I know what happens . . ."

"Do you?"

She looked at me with grim determination. "I close my eyes, and the next face I see is the face of Jesus."

"And you know that? You know that one-hundred percent?"
She nodded.

"And what about the angels?"
She looked slightly puzzled. "The angels will be there."

"Do you feel them?"

Her looked of puzzlement deepened. "Not so much ... but ... but I know they're there."

I squeezed her hand. "Do you feel them like this?"

"Don't be silly," she griped.

"Then how do you really know? How do you really know about angels or about all that other stuff?"

"I can't believe you're talking like this. You're not an atheist all of a sudden, are you?"

"No. No, of course not—just for the sake of argument—"

"You love to argue."

"Just hear me out. Let's say I'm an unbeliever. Let's say I'm a dyed-in-the-wool pagan from Borneo. Tell me how you know about things like angels. Tell me. Humor me."

She sighed. "I just know."

"Tell me how you came to just know."

"I have faith. Faith. Faith in things unseen."

"What if ... what if you had the chance to talk to an angel. Would you take it?"

"Of course."

"You would?"

"I'd love to. We'd all love to. What are you getting at?" Irritated, "Do you have a point?"

"No ... nothing special ... I just wonder why ... I just ..."

"Oh, you're always wondering why. You're—" she gasped. "Why do you always have to plow through life as though no one has been here ahead of you? Why can't you accept things? Ever since you were knee-high to a toadstool, you had to know how electricity traveled through a wire or why the sky was blue or what color God's hair was ... You were always, forever asking Poppie one question after another. And you were never satisfied with the answer. An answer of his would just lead you to another question: 'Why is the sky blue?' you'd ask. 'Because it reflects the ocean,' Poppie would say. And then you'd ask, 'Why is the ocean blue?' It could go on for hours. You have to accept that there are things you'll never know the answer to. Why do I believe in angels? I read about them in the Bible. Poppie and Mama told me they exist. What else do you need?"

"OK, so you have faith," I said.

"Yes."

"But you'd still love to talk to an angel, get the answers to things. Straight from the horse's mouth."

"Of course."

"So what that means is, faith is a pretty poor substitute for the real thing. For really knowing."

She snapped at me, "Don't say things like that. Don't be flip about things that are really very, very important. You're like those people who Paul writes about, people who mock what they cannot understand."

I looked at her as she pulled her thin night coat around her and sat back in the pillows grumpily. My words had hurt her. Maybe scared her. She coughed, and I could almost picture the cancer inside her, clinging to the inside of her lung like a cluster of rotten grapes.

It was important. This was nothing to joke around about.

"I'm sorry," I said. "You're right."

CHAPTER
24

That night I had a fever in my brain. I kept thinking about Peggy's cancer. I kept thinking about Wex. I wanted to get my hands on the angel board, and as soon as I got home, I called Gemma.

She was worn out after another performance of Macbeth.

I told her about Peggy's cancer. Gemma was deeply affected by the news. I thought she was going to start crying. There were long silences, and I filled those silences talking about Peggy's ideas about faith and angels and of certainty and faith.

"When can we get together?" I asked her, referring to the angel board. I knew I was being too pushy. I knew I sounded like a junkie.

There was a long pause. "Merideth, I want to give the angel board a rest for a while," she said. "OK?"

"Why?" pleading.

"I don't completely understand it, and quiet honestly, it scares me a little bit."

"Why does it scare you? I thought this was your thing."

"Well," she said. "Oh ... I guess I'll just tell you. I'm sorry about this, Merideth."

"Sorry about what?"

"Oh, I just got so ... so afraid the other night." Her voice was growing thin and frightened.

"Why?"

"Well, I cheated a little bit. I—"

"Did you move the planchette?" I asked.

"Yes, but only once and only a little bit, and I did it because it seemed so ominous."

"What? What seemed ominous?"

"Well, I played dumb, I guess. I pretended not to know what the board was spelling out when you asked it about your sister, Peggy. The board spelled out P-W-I-L-D-I-E-T. And we decided that that was 'Peggy will diet.' But that's not what the board really spelled. It had stopped on the E, Merideth. And I knew what that meant. The message was "Peggy will die." And I got scared. I got scared, and I bumped the thing just a little so it spelled out diet instead. Peggy will diet. I'm sorry . . . I'm sorry, Merideth, I shouldn't have told you. I know I shouldn't have, not when you've just gotten this news."

"Oh boy . . ." I murmured. I felt a sickness overwhelm me. For the second time that night I was stunned into wordlessness.

"Merideth?" Gemma asked. There was a long, troubled silence. "You know these things aren't necessarily true. I mean, the future is never in a fixed position."

"You mean we always have wiggle room," I said.

"Yes, yes, of course."

"It really spelled that out?" I asked.

"Don't you remember? It stopped on the E, and then at the last second it spilled over to the T. And then you asked if it was a joke. You thought it was a joke."

"And it answered 'No,'" I said.

"Right," she sighed. "The future isn't set in stone."

"Were we in touch with Wex that night?"

"I don't know. We didn't ask for any names."

"OK."

"I'm sorry," she said. "I wasn't going to say anything."

"I might've done the same thing," I said. "Oh, boy," I sighed with weariness.

"I need to go," she said. "I'm just beat. I'm sorry, Merideth. I feel like I've upset you."

"It's all right," I said. "You thought you were doing the right thing."

We exchanged a few more words, and then she hung up, grateful to be off to bed.

My little apartment was very quiet. Green Ash is not a big town, and when all the stores close and all the people are tucked in their beds, the place is as quiet as a mausoleum.

I had that fever in my brain more than ever. Peggy will die. I had more questions now than before—and there was no way I was going to get hold of the angel board . . . not tonight . . .

My eyes went to the closet. There was a moment's tug-of-war in my heart. But in an instant, I was reaching into the upper shelf and pulling down that antique Ouija board.

I opened the long, flat lid and pulled the heavy, wooden board out. I laid it out on the coffee table and then went about the apartment and gathered up three candles. I set them up around the board and then lighted them and turned off the overhead light.

The room was now reduced to a little orange-colored space illuminated by the medieval light of candles. Everything else outside the candle space was veiled in the black of night. I might have been in a witch's cave a thousand years ago.

I took a breath and tried to clear my thoughts, buzzing like hornets inside my skull.

Gemma's warning came back to me—*they say not to do the Ouija board alone.*

This board is powerful, can you feel it?

But I had to. I was aching to reach back out into the unknown.

Before I even started, I knew there was an "other" with me.

I hadn't formally invited anyone in yet that evening. I hadn't touched the planchette . . . yet I could feel a presence, more palpably than ever before. Not just energy in my hands as in past board sessions, not just some vague dreamlike sensation of an "other."

Someone was in the room. Or something.

This board is powerful, can you feel it?

I was aware that there was a breeze outside that was turning to a wind. Shadows of tree branches moved about in my window frame, and beyond the trees a night of fog was dimly lighted by moonglow.

That presence was so very much with me. It was the same sensation from my girlhood that night long ago lying in my bed and hearing my Poppie's voice calling my name. He'd been buried more than a week, and his voice was soft and urgent, coming to me from the hallway.

I had felt a presence then. As surely as if a person were standing in the shadows. Just out of view.

I could leave. Right now I could leave, I thought. Perhaps if I left . . . perhaps if I left, I could pretend I'd never noticed "it."

I went to the trouble of finding my car keys and stuffing them in my pocket.

But I couldn't leave.

It's not that I didn't want to. I couldn't.

It wouldn't let me.

The board was sitting there in the middle of all that golden candle-light. It was waiting for me.

And the "other" was waiting for me. Waiting to communicate with me in its silent, mechanical way.

My mouth was dry and sticky, and my throat tasted of acid.

Submitting to the silent beckon, I sat back down in front of the board.

I didn't want to be there. I felt an oily, perverse presence. An ancient, intelligent, insectlike being. There in the room. Watching invisibly.

I placed my nervous fingers lightly on the planchette. It felt different than Gemma's. It was made of wood, not plastic. And the board had a different feel. A strong magnetism. It had an old soul. It was aged, and the varnish was shiny and filled with a spider web of cracks, and in the center instead of the handsome angel, there was that magician with the Egyptian face. The red stone in the magician's eye glinted every so often in the candlelight. As their little flames grew and fell.

I took a long breath. I was telling myself that the presence was an angel and wasn't I lucky? Wasn't I fortunate to be visited in this way?

"Good evening," I said, and the planchette slipped quietly to *Hello.*

I caught my breath. My heart was pounding against my ribs like a startled bird in a cage.

Any final suspicions I'd held in reserve that Gemma was moving the planchette were gone.

It was moving. The board was alive.

This session was so different from the others. I was meeting a challenge. Or a threat. I had no human companion. I was alone and in a place where I couldn't call for help.

Alone with my unseen, unnatural guest.

"Is this Wex?" I asked aloud. My voice sounded foreign to me, like it was not my own.

No, came the reply.

I decided to try again. "Is this Wex?"

Yes, came the perplexing reply and then, just as I was ready to take my fingers off the planchette, it shot over to *No.*

No. Yes. No.

My mouth was dry. My eyes were beginning to water.

"I want to speak to Wex," I said, my voice faltering.

The planchette made a deft move. *No.*

One of the candles winked and then went out. It made a soft hissing as the wick was overwhelmed by hot wax.

Someone was playing with me. I needed the lights to be on. Somehow if the lights were on, I'd feel safer. But I couldn't leave the board.

I was in over my head. I could feel it. I had invited something in.

"I am surrounded by the white light," I said, trembling. "I want to talk to an angel."

No, came the reply.

"I want to talk to an angel," I commanded.

This time the board spelled out G...O...T...O...H...E...L...

Another candle went out. The sharp smell of wax smoke in my nostrils.

My shaking hands went to my mouth. My chin felt twisted up, just as it does before you sob. My throat was hard and choking, like just before you vomit. This thing hated me.

I felt its cold, hard hatred.

"I am a child of God," I said, my teeth chattering, placing shivering fingers on the planchette. "I want ... to t-t-talk to an ... angel."

The room was freezing cold.

Only one candle was still burning. Its flame lengthened into a sharp point.

I had not pulled the planchette back to the center, but it moved again and it spelled R...O...S...E...

"Rose," I whimpered. What a colossal insult. My throat hurt; it was convulsing, and I thought it would burst open.

"This isn't you ..."

Yes, the planchette replied.

Tears began to sting in my eyes.

"This can't be you ... it can't ... this is a demon!"

The planchette moved to *Hello.*

Terror brushed lightly up the back of my neck.

The room was growing smaller and liquid.

I felt the presence grow more powerful on my fear. It seemed to slurp up my fear. To draw strength from it. It was toying with me. Like a vampire, sucking the horror right out of me, feeding itself. Pretending to be my Rose, opening up the deepest wound inside me. Going straight for my heart muscle.

"You're not Rose," I wept.

I had taken my fingers off the planchette, clutching myself, shivering uncontrollably, but still it moved. The planchette jittered around the board aimlessly like a wind-up spider.

"You're not my Rose," I wept, weak with terror.

The last candle blinked out.

A voice spoke: "Yes."

I screamed and clamped my hand to my mouth. A voice had spoken. Hissed out of the shadows—there'd been a breathy, audible response.

"You're not Rose!" I wailed.

And I saw it.

A figure. In a deep shadow in the far corner. An erect, black figure seated in a chair near the window. Watching me.

It had a large, smooth head and wide shoulders. Hunched forward.

"Oh, God, please!" I cried out. I went faint. I felt my legs give out from beneath me. I stumbled to the floor and scrambled on my hands and knees. The door was miles away.

I could feel that black figure staring at me. I thought I heard it speak again. It was there with me. In the visible world—I had invited it here. I had somehow given it passage into our world. I had fed it with my ignorance and with my pride and fear.

Was it rising? Was it going to come after me?

"Oh, God, dear God!" I wept. I was blinded by tears, scrambling, standing, and falling. My hair sticking to my wet eyes.

And in a moment I was outside. In the foggy darkness, in the chill.

"Oh, Jesus, please save me, please protect me. Dear Jesus, please save me. Please, please, please don't leave me."

Even though I was outside, I still felt it with me—that figure of blackness. I felt it had attached itself to me. And I fell to my knees outside my car. And I prayed harder and with more belief than I'd ever prayed before. I don't remember the words, I only knew that my only hope was in the God of my fathers. I felt so close to a breakdown, to madness.

For the first time, I knew what real evil felt like.

I had long ago sensed a tiny hint of it, staring death in the face while clinging to the edge of a casket. That tiny opening in the fabric between real good and real evil.

Death is so empty, such a cold, feelingless insult to life. And it was as if the figure of unrighteous death itself had appeared before me.

Now I was on the ground, pleading with God. Crying out like an animal. I had no questions. There was no room for debate.

I needed protection. I needed it now, or I would lose my mind.

I had thrown back a thin sheet between this world and a world of evil. And I knew, finally, absolutely knew, that only God's love and strength stands between us and a legion of demons. Demons without faces, without humor, without warmth.

I dug my car keys out of my pocket, and at last I was able to pull myself into my car, and I drove slowly, almost too weak to drive, over to Peggy and Brenda Ann's house.

The house was dark, and everyone was asleep when I arrived. I let myself in, and I went to Poppie's study, and I turned all the lights on. I sat with his old Bible, in his old chair, under that ancient painting of the family who gazed up toward heaven. And I prayed like I had not prayed since childhood.

I put my head on the desk . . . exhausted. I just slumped there, praying to make it through the night.

At some point, I drifted off to sleep. And I had a succession of vivid dreams.

In one I was in a house, like the schoolhouse, only it was larger, and all the reconstruction was finished. Marc was there, and Poppie was there, and they were looking the place over saying something about tearing it down. "But this house is my life," I said. But they told me that a demon had gotten loose in the house, and you had to tear a place down when that happened. I remember someone had used the toilet. And it would flush. And then the bowl would fill again with urine, and then it would flush again, and then it would refill. "See, we've got to start from scratch," a voice said.

And then I was in a car driving down the coast highway, and I was hit head-on by a gigantic truck. And I managed to crawl from the wreckage through smoke and fire, and I remember shouting, "I have to talk to God! I have to talk to God!" But no one knew how I could do that.

And I was running down the road, and I finally came to a tele-
phone booth, and I dialed the operator, and I was begging her, I said,
"I have to talk to God," and she said, "Just one moment, please." And
I knew I wasn't going to be able to talk to Him. I waited and waited.
And she came back on, and she said, "I'm sorry, you'll have to call
back. He's very busy." And I was frantic, and I pleaded with her, and
all she'd say was, "I'm sorry, you'll have to call back."

In the dream I was beyond consolation. I felt lost. Eternally lost. I
felt as though I was losing my mind and that at any moment I would
die and spend all eternity in demon-ravaged darkness.

I left the phone booth, and I walked back to the wreck, and everyone was gone. The scene was utterly deserted. Smoke curled up out
of the crash. And I just stood there looking at the wreckage of my
car and the truck and thinking about my father and Marc tearing
down the schoolhouse. And then ...

I can hardly describe what happened next.

I saw someone. I saw a man who was in regular street clothes. He
had the spring and bounce of youth, but I couldn't place his age. He
had kind of long hair, and he had a nice jean jacket on, and he had a
face of such sunny warmth. Such kind, gentle, loving eyes. And I
recognized him. Immediately recognized him. He had the most familiar face.

I have seen him before. Maybe in dreams. Maybe on the street,
but I knew him. I've seen him a thousand times in a thousand different places. I will always know that this was a real angel. This was the
angel who's been with me all my life.

Such a sense of relief passed through me. As though every muscle
in my body relaxed at the same time.

He came up to me, and what he said was very simple.

"It's going to be OK," he said, in a voice of simple comfort.

And when he said it, I knew it was true.

Then he touched me on the arm, and he smiled in a slightly sad
way, a thoughtful way, and he said, "Don't do those things."

And I knew what he meant.

That's all he needed to say. It was enough. And because he said it,
I felt peace. I knew all that I needed to know.

When I woke up, I knew what pure good was. I knew the depths
of its kindness, its gentleness, its forgiveness, its faithfulness. And I

knew the distance between what is good and what is evil. Because I had traveled that distance in the course of a sudden, single night.

Some people have suggested that I had probably seen a shadow that night in my apartment and that the voice I heard was simply the wind scratching against my window. And I can't argue with that. I don't know everything. All I know is what I experienced, what I saw and felt. It changed me. It clarified my mind. It made me believe in things unseen. It made me believe in angels—angels of light and of darkness. And it made me believe in the power of prayer.

The next day I drove out to the lonely, desolate spot where Rose and my Poppie and Mama and little Sammy Boy were all buried. The sun was hidden behind a vast shield of gray clouds that stretched out over the iron-gray sea. But I didn't feel melancholy. I didn't feel the emptiness of death this time. I didn't feel angry at God. Instead, for the first time, I felt the determined hope of a future together, a someday in which we could all join hands again and look toward an eternity with our God.

I felt the solemn stirring of a new faith in things outside of the visible realm. In new roses. In a new heaven and a new earth.

Epilogue

"I have a hard head. The only lessons I've ever learned are the ones imprinted on a two-by-four, which was then thwacked across the top of my skull," I said to Brenda Ann.

The sun was bright gold in a terrifically blue sky. We stood side by side outside the schoolhouse watching the fire burn. Bit by bit we were tossing all kinds of junk into the flames—pieces of old rotten flooring, shingles, other garbage from the yet-to-be-completed schoolhouse renovation.

The flames had gobbled up the old Ouija board quickly. Brenda Ann had been fearful that it might not burn. Or worse, that it might let out a scream in the flames.

None of that happened. We'd said a quick prayer, spit on it, and given it the old heave-ho. That's all that was required.

Now the flames crackled and snapped, and smoke rose hastily into the air over our heads.

"I just can't believe how far you went with it," she said, continuing our conversation about the angel board and Ouija.

"I know."

"Didn't it scare you?"

"Yes, at first. But that just made me mad as a wet hen. I hate to be scared of anything."

Brenda Ann put her arm around me and gave me a quick kiss. "Sometimes," she sighed, "you're not very bright."

"I know," I said. "I'm not a big, smart person."

"That's what mom says about herself."

"She's right about some things."

"Yeah." She nodded and patted me on the back. "You know, I've gotta go. I promised I'd read to her this afternoon."

"OK. She seems all right," I said, hopefully. "Considering . . ."

"Yeah, the doctor thinks they may've gotten it in time," Brenda Ann said. She bit her lip and squinted in the glare of the sun. "She'll have to undergo some chemotherapy, but the doctor seemed pretty upbeat. She's stronger than I'd ever known."

"She's been through a lot in her life."

"She has," Brenda Ann agreed. "And if the doctor's not a complete flake, I think she may get through this too."

I nodded. "Good. That's good news."

"Marc is going to have a prayer service at the hospital."

"He called and told me," I nodded, "Tomorrow at noon?"

"Yeah."

I gave her a kiss. "I'll be there, hon."

"Thanks."

She got in her car and drove slowly down the gravel lane; just before her car made the bend, she honked once and waved. I waved back.

I spent much of the afternoon cleaning up around the schoolhouse, throwing more old, burnable junk on the fire. This was the sweat part of sweat equity you put into a project like this.

And it gave me time to think. Time to sort through thoughts like, "Where do I go from here?"

Around seven that evening, I sat on the front steps with a paper bag. I had a sandwich inside and a couple peaches—we were getting good peaches that year.

The sandwich was made from thick bread, and it was composed of things I'd found in Peggy's refrigerator: pickles and cheese and bell peppers. I was so hungry from an afternoon of what used to be called honest labor; that sandwich was about the best thing I'd ever eaten. And the peaches—wow—that first juicy bite, and my dry mouth was filled with joy.

As I sat there eating, enjoying the onset of twilight, I heard the sound of a car, and I looked over, and there was Dan Hanson driving carefully up my little lane.

Epilogue

My stomach did a little flip.

He had a funny, quiet smile on his face, and he came up and gave me a hug. He was looking his usual lanky, good-looking, wind-strewn self.

"Have a seat, professor," I said, patting the step beside me.

"I don't want to interrupt your dinner."

"Oh, sure you do."

He sat next to me, and we chatted a bit.

"Did Brenda Ann put you up to this?" I asked.

He laughed, showing all his pretty teeth. "Yeah, I guess she did," he admitted.

"She's not all bad."

The sun was hot orange and simmering away down at the horizon on the far side of the ocean. And one by one, stars were appearing in the darkening sky. I remembered once that Dan had told me that when his wife left him, he'd gone away to a place where he could pray and contemplate. That said to me that this was a guy who didn't let his science get in the way of his heart.

It made me think that we might be able to make more than just small talk.

Getting to know people is all about taking chances. So . . .

"So when you look in the sky at night, Dan Hanson—Mr. Astronomer, what do you see? You being a man of science and all."

I offered him half of a peach, and he accepted it. He was quiet for a moment, eating slowly. "Well, as a man of science, I see orbs of fiery gasses. Hydrogen mostly, all spinning around and around. But that's only part of it. That's the textbook answer."

"What's the real answer?" I asked.

"The real answer . . . well, when I was a boy and lived way out in the boonies of Arkansas, I used to like to do those connect-the-dot drawings."

"Uh-huh."

"And on nights light this, I'd lay down in my front yard, and I'd listen to the katydids, and I'd look up past the fireflies up to the stars. And when you live out in the country like that, the stars look different. They kind of look like someone's spilled heaps of diamonds on a blackboard. And I'd stare up at them just knowing—convinced!—that I was looking at a big dot-to-dot puzzle. I was sure that if I could connect them right, I might see a message spelled out. Some kind of

187

important message from God Himself. And I spent a lot of time do-ing that, trying to connect the dots."

I liked that. I thought about it awhile. "And what do you see now that you're all grown up? Do you just see fiery orbs?"

He took my hand and he said, "No, I see a message . . ." as though that was the most obvious thing a person could say.

"What's the message?" I asked.

"Oh, it changes," he said. "It's different every night. That's why you have to come out to a place like this, and you have to sit quietly and maybe eat a peach or something, and you have to see what's what."

"I see what you mean."

"Do you?"

"Sure. I can tell you what the message is."

"Oh, you can. That was fast."

"The message tonight . . ." I paused. "The message tonight is 'listen up, you!'"

"Really."

"Yeah. Maybe not that gruff. But that's it." I pointed up into the increasingly star-populated sky. "See, there's the L and the I and the S . . . it spells it all out. 'Listen up, you!' That's the message."

He nodded.

I turned to Dan Hanson. "What did you think the message was?"

He made a noncommittal *hmmmming* sound. "I don't know yet," he said. "You have to give me a minute. It takes me longer."

"Take all the time you want."

We sat out there under the growing canopy of stars for a long, long time talking quietly, and I told him all about the tarot cards and the angel board and the Ouija board—even at that moment a part of the glowing, popping pile of embers. I tried to tell him about seeing evil and seeing good, but I'm not always good with words. I felt my tongue getting all twisted around.

He said he understood, though.

I told him maybe I'd try to write it out. Maybe if I could sit down and think about it slowly and carefully, then maybe I could convey some of what had taken me on that long, strange journey.

He told me he'd read something by an old-time shrink named Carl Jung who said something like, "The right way to wholeness is, unfortunately, a twisted path sometimes thick with horrors." I'm paraphrasing.

"Maybe you've gone through a dark time so you can more fully appreciate the light," he said.

"That's awfully poetic," I said, teasing him.

I saw him smile patiently in the darkness. "Listen up, you."

"So is that the message tonight?" I asked.

"Just wait," he said. "Just be quiet for one minute. Can you do that?"

"I can do that."

"Just try it. You'll get all the answers you need. Just be quiet . . . just listen."

"OK, here goes . . ." I tried. Quietly.

"Are you listening?" he asked.

"Wait a minute," I whispered. "Are we listening, or are we connecting the dots?"

"Both," he said. "If you're quiet, then you can see better."

I wasn't sure what he meant, but I knew that I had a lot yet to learn.

For some reason, I remembered a flash from my dream a few nights previous in which my Poppie and Marc were talking about tearing down the schoolhouse and I had cried, "But it's my life!"

Funny how your mind latches onto symbols like that. Because that old schoolhouse was very much my life. Historic. Full of holes. In need of a solid foundation. In need of windows to let in light. In need of a master carpenter's touch.

And as I gazed up into God's starry, secret alphabet, I realized that for an ex-real estate agent headed into menopause, I still had a lot of life ahead of me. And a lot of life means a lot more bends in the road, new lessons to learn, new guidance to seek.

I was warmly comforted that in spite of all my chicanery and foolishness, I'd never been forsaken by the God who's put together this spectacular starry, starry night.

There would be other mistakes, and there would be other narrow escapes from stupidity. But there's God, who is good and who gives us wiggle room. We all need wiggle room.

IF YOU ENJOYED THIS BOOK...

you might enjoy reading other books in our Sycamore Tree line.

Prayer Warriors
Guardians
Eleventh Hour
Midnight Hour
Be My Angel
It's Time to Stop Rehearsing What We Believe
The Journal of a Not-So-Perfect Daughter

Turn the page to find out more.

IT'S TIME TO STOP REHEARSING WHAT WE BELIEVE AND START LOOKING AT WHAT DIFFERENCE IT MAKES

Reinder Bruinsma

Finally, a book that answers the question "What difference does it make?" Even if you've grown up in the church and taken all the religion classes, sometimes there seems to be more questions than answers. Does what we believe really matter in the way we live? Does being an Adventist go beyond being in church on Saturday monring?

With stories and illustrations that bring the book to life, Reinder Bruinsma, a long-time church pastor and administrator, honestly and clearly explores the purpose and value of each of our doctrines.

ISBN: 0-8163-1401-2. US$9.99, Can$14.49.

ELEVENTH HOUR

Céleste perrino Walker and Eric Stoffle

A religious coalition with a strong political agenda. A movement for all churches to "get together." Believers doubting whether or not holding onto a few "different" beliefs is worth being ridiculed by the world—especially by other Christians. Strange, incurable plagues.

A new end-time story? Or headlines from today's newspapers? *Eleventh Hour* is the story of a father searching for his lost daughter, a doctor searching for a cure. It is the story of a man who believes he is working for God in a political movement. It is the story of an FBI agent working deep undercover and his sister's struggle with addiction—and with the challenge of accepting the truth.

ISBN: 0-8163-1649-X. US$12.99, Can$18.99.

MIDNIGHT HOUR

Céleste perrino Walker and Eric Stoffle

The exciting sequel to *Eleventh Hour*. With time winding down, the world hurtles toward certain destruction. But whle the wicked seek to blame and destroy the Remnant for their misery, God's faithful discover peace, hope, and courage. Whose side will you be on just minutes to Midnight?

ISBN: 0-8163-1698-8. US$12.99, Can$18.99.